DISASTER

The twins were in a corner by themselves, not even talking with their Fairfield friends. Marie sat by herself also, and the other girls simply paired up, old friend with old friend. The party had Failure written all over it.

"Come on, Sara," Darcy said, sure if she got Sara going, the party would fall into shape. "Talk with the twins. They're really interesting once you get to know them."

"They don't look interesting," Sara declared. "Just weird."

"They do look strange," Jessica said. "Not interested in anyone but themselves."

"Fairfield girls are always just interested in themselves," Sara said. "Rich snobby girls are like that."

Darcy sighed. The last thing the party needed was Sara broadcasting her opinion of Fairfield girls. She edged away from Sara and Jessica, and prayed that April could think of something before open hostilities broke out. Not that April was trying to get her friends to cooperate. She was standing by herself, not talking to anyone. Some co-hostess she was turning out to be. . . .

Other Bantam Skylark Books you will enjoy
Ask your bookseller for the books you have missed

ANYTHING FOR A FRIEND by Ellen Conford

APRIL UPSTAIRS by Susan Beth Pfeffer

DAPHNE'S BOOK by Mary Downing Hahn

DEAR CELESTE, MY LIFE IS A MESS
by Francess Lantz

FELITA by Nicholasa Mohr

FREUD AND FREUD, INC. by Carole Mohr

THE GHOST CHILDREN by Eve Bunting

THE GHOST WORE GRAY by Bruce Coville

KANGAROO KIDS by Patricia Bernard

THE TRUTH ABOUT TAFFY SINCLAIR
by Betsy Haynes

YEARBOOK MEMORIES (The Fabulous Five Super
Edition #4) by Betsy Haynes

Susan Beth Pfeffer

DARCY DOWNSTAIRS

A BANTAM SKYLARK BOOK
NEW YORK · TORONTO · LONDON · SYDNEY · AUCKLAND

This edition contains the complete text
of the original hardcover edition.
NOT ONE WORD HAS BEEN OMITTED.

RL 6, 008–012

DARCY DOWNSTAIRS

A Bantam Skylark Book / published by arrangement with
Henry Holt and Company, Inc.

PUBLISHING HISTORY
Henry Holt edition published 1990
Bantam edition / January 1993

Skylark Books is a registered trademark of Bantam Books,
a division of Bantam Doubleday Dell Publishing Group, Inc.
Registered in U.S. Patent and Trademark Office and elsewhere.

ISBN 0-553-15942-9

Published simultaneously in the United States and Canada

Bantam Books are published by Bantam Books, a division of Bantam
Doubleday Dell Publishing Group, Inc. Its trademark, consisting of the
words "Bantam Books" and the portrayal of a rooster, is Registered in
U.S. Patent and Trademark Office and in other countries. Marca
Registrada. Bantam Books, 666 Fifth Avenue, New York, New York
10103.

PRINTED IN THE UNITED STATES OF AMERICA

OPM   0 9 8 7 6 5 4 3 2 1

For the Writing Group:
Pat George,
Bonnie Kraham,
Pam Mather-Kathy,
and Hilarie Staton

DARCY DOWNSTAIRS

ONE

Tap tap tap tap tap.

No, that wouldn't work.

Tap. Tap tap. Tap. Tap.

Better, but still not perfect.

"Hello, Darcy. What are you up to?"

"Oh, hi, Mayor Beckstein," Darcy Greene said from behind the counter at her parents' shop, Video To Go. "I'm tapping."

"I guessed that," the mayor said with a smile. "What are you tapping about?"

"I'm trying to work out a code," Darcy replied. "My cousin April lives upstairs from me, and her bedroom is right over my bedroom—well, half my bedroom, and half my sister Isabelle's—and it seemed to me if April and I could just work out a tapping code, we wouldn't have to talk on the phone so much. My sister Isabelle would prefer it if we didn't. Not that she gets that many phone calls, but she says it's because April and I are always on the phone, and we should just move in together if we want to talk that much. Only we can't do that. There isn't enough room in my room for her, and I don't want to leave my parents, not even to go upstairs. So I'm tapping. Do you know what movie you want to take out?''

"I'm not sure," Mayor Beckstein said. "I was going to ask your mother for advice. She always knows just the right movie for me."

"She's at the dentist," Darcy said. "She should be back in a couple of minutes. Dad's in the back room going over order forms. I can get him if you want to take out something X-rated."

"No, that's all right," Mayor Beckstein said. "I'm more the PG-13 type myself."

"That's a good rating," Darcy said. "Have you seen *Free Fall* yet? It's PG-13 and very funny. We got it in a couple of days ago, but one just came back if you want to take it out."

"*Free Fall,*" the mayor said. "You know, I heard that was a nice comedy. Maybe that's what I'm in the mood for."

"We saw it over the weekend," Darcy said. "And even Isabelle laughed. She never laughs, because she's a poet. She says poets have to be serious about nearly everything."

"So do mayors," Mayor Beckstein declared. "I think I'll take out *Free Fall*. Thank you, Darcy."

"You're welcome," Darcy said, taking the mayor's card out of the file and giving it to her to sign.

"So," Mayor Beckstein said as Darcy handed her the videotape. "Do you like having your cousin live in the same house as you?"

"I love it," Darcy replied. "She and I are just about the exact same age. April goes to Fairfield. Maybe you saw her on TV. She interviewed Lyon Fitzhugh, the rock star, right before his airplane went down in Africa. Then, when they found him, April got to be on TV. She was real famous for about a week last month."

"About a week sounds like just the right amount of time to be famous," the mayor said. "Longer than that, and you might get bored."

"I'm going to be famous for a lot longer than a week," Darcy declared. "Once I'm a great film director, I expect to be famous for years and years. Then I'm going to retire young and devote myself to worthy causes. But I guess I'll stay famous. I don't think fame stops just because you're being noble all the time."

"It sounds like you have your life all mapped out," the mayor said.

"Of course I do," Darcy replied. "So does Isabelle. She's going to be a poet, and I get to support her. Don't you have your life mapped out? Mayor today, governor in a year or two, and then president?"

The mayor laughed. "I haven't gotten past mayor," she said. "And I never fantasize past state senator."

"I guess you're already famous," Darcy said. "Being

mayor and all. Maybe someday I'll make a movie based on your life. Would you like that?"

"Only if it's rated PG-13," the mayor said. "Thanks, Darcy. I'll let you know how much I like the movie."

"See you soon," Darcy said. As soon as the mayor left, Darcy returned to her tapping. Of course, a pencil against a counter wasn't the same as a broom handle against a ceiling, but it was all Darcy needed to make up a code.

Tap. Tap tap tap. Tap. Tap.

That was good. That could stand for "I had a good day at school. How about you?"

Darcy grabbed a piece of paper out of her notebook and wrote down the number of taps and what they meant.

Tap. Tap. Tap tap.

That meant "It was okay." Or maybe it should just mean "Okay" for any question. "How are you?" *Tap. Tap. Tap tap.* "Want to watch some TV together?" *Tap. Tap. Tap tap.*

Of course, if all they wanted to say was "Yes," then why have all those taps? In the movies it was always one blink for yes and two for no, or maybe the other way around. But it was never four blinks with pauses in between. Darcy was glad film directors didn't have to make codes, too.

The bell rang, indicating someone had entered the store, so Darcy looked up. It was her mother.

"I'm back," she said. "Complete with dazzling teeth." She smiled broadly so Darcy could admire them.

"How many cavities?" Darcy asked.

"None," her mother replied. "Grown-ups don't get cavities. They get root canals and gum diseases and bridgework, but they never get cavities."

"I think I'd rather get cavities," Darcy said.

"You're a smart kid," her mother said. "Thanks for store-sitting. Have things been busy?"

"Not really," Darcy said. "Maybe a half dozen people. Nobody asked for anything X-rated, so Dad stayed in the back the whole time."

"Good," her mother said. "He has a lot of paperwork to catch up on."

Darcy considered asking her mother about tapping codes, but it seemed to her the kind of thing parents were best left out of. You never knew when they were going to be sensitive about broom handles and ceilings.

The doorbell rang again, and when Darcy looked at the door, she saw her best friend Sara come in.

"Hi, Darcy," Sara said. "I was at the library."

Video To Go was a couple of blocks away from the library, going toward Sara's house, so it made sense she'd drop in. "Did you take out anything good?" Darcy asked.

"I got a book for that book report we have due," Sara said. "A week from Friday. I figured if I took the book out now, maybe I'd get it read before the weekend, and I could write the report then and not have to worry about it all next week."

"That sounds very efficient, Sara," Darcy's mother declared. "I wish I was that organized."

"My mother says if you have four kids and a full-time job and a husband who never picks up after himself, you have to be organized," Sara replied. "Or crazy. Sometimes she says one and sometimes the other. I think she means both. Darcy, do you want to have supper at my house? I asked Mom if I could ask you, and she said sure, why not, what's another empty, gaping mouth. We're having codfish balls. They really stink, so if you have some, we'll all have fewer we have to eat, and then maybe Mom'll give us more dessert to compensate. Tommy's bringing home three of his friends, and two of them don't even mind codfish balls. I think they have dead tastebuds."

"You don't want too many people," Darcy said. "Or else there might not be enough dessert."

"We always have enough dessert," Sara said. "Mom doesn't much like codfish balls either. She only makes them because her mother made them, and she says if she had to suffer through them in her childhood, so do we. So she always buys ice-cream cake on codfish-ball night as a reward."

"How many codfish balls would I have to eat?" Darcy asked. Ice-cream cake did sound tempting.

"No more than two," Sara said. "Maybe just one, if Tommy's friends come through the way he said they

[6]

would. We also have rice and cauliflower, so it looks like there's stuff on your plate even when there isn't."

"Can I?" Darcy asked her mother.

"Have you done your homework?" Darcy's mother asked.

"Not yet," Darcy admitted. "But I could do it after I got home from Sara's."

"I don't think so," her mother said. "I think the codfish balls will have to wait until some night when we have a little more advance warning."

"Okay," Sara said. "Maybe I can get my baby brother Mikey to eat my share. He's just starting to eat real foods, and anything's got to be better than that strained stuff they've been giving him."

"Next time," Darcy said.

"I'd better go," Sara said. "See you in school tomorrow."

"Sure," Darcy said. "Bye."

Darcy's mother shuddered. "Codfish balls," she said. "They sound awful."

"Yeah," Darcy said. "But the ice-cream cake sounded really good."

"It did, didn't it?" her mother said. "Maybe I'll get one for us this weekend. Joanne and April could help us eat it."

"That'd be great," Darcy said.

"Speaking of undone homework," her mother said. "Do you want to get home and start doing it?"

"Okay," Darcy said, but before she'd had a chance

to gather her schoolbooks together, the door opened again and in walked April.

"Hi," she said. "I was on my way to the library, and I thought I'd see how your dentist appointment went, Aunt Karen."

"No cavities," Darcy's mother replied. "Clean, sound, healthy teeth."

"Congratulations," April said. "Mom always says people with good teeth are healthier than people with rotting ones. I have a book report due next week, so I figured I'd take something out and start reading it. Wanna come, Darcy?"

"Sure," Darcy said. "I'll go straight home from the library, Mom, and start on my homework then."

"Take a book out for your own book report," her mother said. "Try to get the same head start on it Sara has."

"Okay," Darcy said, and as soon as she said it, she thought *Tap. Tap. Tap tap,* and giggled. "Come on, April. What kind of book do you have to read?"

"It doesn't matter what kind," April said as she and Darcy walked out of the store. "Just as long as it's a hundred and twenty pages or more."

"I think that's what I have to read too," Darcy said. "How was school?"

"It was okay," April said. "We had a meeting of the *Fairfield Forward.* That's why I was late. I wanted to visit with you in the store until Aunt Karen got back, but I just left school a few minutes ago."

"That's okay," Darcy said. "I had a lot to keep me busy. Did they give you any good assignments?"

April shook her head. "I didn't like any of the stuff they needed articles about," she said. "And I have this book report to do and an essay for Spanish and a book to read in French, and I just figured I might as well take the month off from journalism. How was your day?"

"It was okay," Darcy said. "We had a surprise quiz in science, but I'd done my homework so I think I got most of it right."

"I still wish sometimes that I went to the Middle School with you," April said, "instead of Fairfield. Do you ever wish you went to Fairfield?"

Darcy shook her head. "The girls there are kind of weird," she said. "Not all of them, I guess, but most of the ones I've met."

"That reminds me," April said. "Megan and Melissa invited me to their house for dinner Saturday night. I'm finally going to meet their father. And they said I should ask you if you could come too. They'd call you themselves, only their father's mad at one of them and he can't remember which, so neither of them are allowed to make phone calls. I said I'd give you the invitation."

"I'd love to go," Darcy said. She'd been intrigued by Megan and Melissa since April had first brought them home. "I can't wait to meet their father and see their house. Do you think their bedrooms are identical the way they are?"

"I'm almost scared to find out," April replied. "I was hoping they'd ask you, too. I didn't want to go there alone the first time. Oh, they said they'd send their chauffeur to pick us up and take us home. That way Mom and your parents won't have to bother."

"I wonder if their father could help me with my career," Darcy said. "He's a big Broadway producer, and they must know lots of great film directors."

"I think he hates the movies," April said. "He says they're killing Broadway. I only hope he doesn't think I'm killing Broadway. He scares me."

"I'll protect you," Darcy said with a giggle. "Sara wanted me to have supper with her family tonight. They're having codfish balls. It'd be funny if that's what we had at Megan and Melissa's."

"I sure hope not," April said. "I hate codfish balls."

"I bet we have something expensive and glamorous," Darcy said. "The kind of stuff they serve on fire."

"That doesn't sound too great either," April said. "Do you know what book you want to take out?"

Darcy shook her head. The girls entered the library and walked directly to the teen section. April went over to the fiction shelves, and Darcy followed her.

"Maybe they have the new Liz Reuben," April said. "She's my absolute favorite."

"I like her stuff too," Darcy said. April walked over to the R authors, but the new Liz Reuben was nowhere to be seen. Darcy waited to see what April's next choice would be.

April took a book off the shelves, examined it, then put it back. She did the same with two more books. Darcy checked out April's rejections, but they didn't appeal to her, either.

"This looks good," April said. "*A Pocketful of Love.*" She pulled the book off the shelf and began reading the book jacket.

"What's it about?" Darcy asked.

"There's a girl and she's fifteen and she's never been in love before," April said. "And then she meets this boy, Terry, and he's real angry because his family doesn't have any money."

"I like stories like that," Darcy said. "How many pages?"

"One hundred and forty-two," April said.

"Maybe I'll take it," Darcy said.

"No fair," April said. "I found it. You find your own book to read."

"Sorry," Darcy said. "I thought you were just thinking about it. I didn't realize you'd already picked it."

"Well, I had," April said. "Besides, you don't like romance books. I've never once seen you read one."

"That's because they always remind me of Isabelle," Darcy replied. "She's so romantic with her poetry."

"You don't have to take out a novel," April said. "There're lots of nonfiction books a hundred and twenty pages long."

Darcy nodded. She walked over to the nonfiction section and began reading the titles.

"Here's one for you," April said. *Direct Your Own Videos.* Let's see. It's a hundred and fifty-four pages long, but it has some pictures and the print's pretty big."

Darcy took the book from her cousin. "I bet there's nothing in there I don't already know," she said.

"Good," April said. "You'll read it a lot faster that way. Come on. Take it out, and then we can go home and try to decide what we should wear on Saturday."

"You mean we have to dress up for this dinner?" Darcy asked as she followed April to the checkout desk.

"The twins are going to," April said. "Blue velvet with Belgian-lace collars."

Darcy shook her head. For an outfit like that, flaming codfish balls were definitely the only right thing to eat.

TWO

Darcy stared down at her tuna-fish sandwich. "I wish my mother could cook," she said.

"You say that every time they make us franks and beans," Sara pointed out. "Which is practically three times a week."

"Only twice a week," Jessica Malone said. "I like their franks and beans. I think it's just about the only thing they serve that's edible."

"It's sure better than my mom's codfish balls," Sara declared. "Why don't you try some, Darcy? Maybe you'll like it after all."

Darcy shook her head. "I ate some when I was in first grade, and I threw up for three days afterward," she declared. "I'm not taking any more chances."

"You did not," Sara said. "It was just one day, and the nurse said you had a twenty-four-hour virus, and you've been blaming it on these poor, innocent franks and beans ever since."

"They get along fine without me, I get along fine without them," Darcy said, then took another bite of her sandwich. "I just wish my mother could cook."

"What's wrong with your sandwich?" Jessica asked.

"Nothing," Darcy said. "I made it. I opened up a can of no-oil, no-salt, no-nothing tuna fish and dumped it on twenty-thousand-grain bread, because we're not allowed to eat white bread anymore, or tuna in oil, now that Aunt Joanne is upstairs, and we don't have mayo in the house either, so I spread some yogurt on the bread, only I think all the grains ate it up, and the sandwich tastes like the Sahara Desert, only worse."

"Yogurt?" Sara said. "On a sandwich?"

"It was that or mustard," Darcy replied. "We don't even have peanut butter around. Aunt Joanne is investigating different brands to see which one has the least fat and flavor."

"You know," Sara said, pushing her franks and beans around on the plate. "That's the first sort-of-bad thing you've said about your aunt Joanne."

"What do you mean?" Darcy asked, then forced herself to take a bite of the worst tuna-fish sandwich ever created.

"All you ever do is say how great it is she lives upstairs from you," Sara replied. "How much fun it is and everything."

"I didn't think I ever talked about Aunt Joanne," Darcy said. "I mean, I love her, but she is just an aunt."

"I think Sara's saying you talk about April all the time," Jessica said. "And how great it is she's living upstairs from you."

"Well, that is great," Darcy said. "She doesn't like the foods her mother buys either. She comes downstairs all the time just to eat cookies and stuff."

"How come your mother still buys cookies if you can't eat white bread?" Jessica asked.

Darcy grinned. "Mom says no sister of hers is going to come between her and chocolate," she replied. "And Dad loves potato chips, so we have those around too, only we hide them from Aunt Joanne. Once, Dad was eating from the bag and Aunt Joanne came down unexpectedly, and Dad hid the entire bag behind him. When she left, he saw he'd crushed every single chip. Things get pretty exciting sometimes."

"Then why do you like having them live there?" Sara asked. "If you can't even eat what you want anymore?"

"It isn't so bad," Darcy said. "And some nights Aunt Joanne does the cooking, and she's really good. The food she makes is good for you, but the way she cooks it, it tastes okay anyway."

"And then you get to eat with your cousin April," Sara said.

"Sure," Darcy said. "It'd be a little weird if Aunt Joanne just cooked for me and not April."

"You do practically everything nowadays with April," Sara said. "Don't you."

Darcy shook her head. "No I don't," she said. "I'm having lunch with the two of you right now, and April isn't around."

"Let's change the subject," Jessica said. "What do you think about that new girl who just started? Marie, I think her name is. She's in my gym class. Do you know who I mean?"

"I bet Darcy wishes she were April," Sara said. "Then they could be having lunch together."

"That isn't exactly changing the subject," Jessica said. "I think Marie seems okay. It must be hard to start a new school in October. I remember when I moved here four years ago, and it was hard enough in September. It's always so weird going to a new school, everybody friends with everybody else already and you don't know anyone yet."

"Is that why you're always doing stuff with April?" Sara asked. "Because she's new and she doesn't have any friends?"

"April has friends," Darcy said. "And I'm not always doing stuff with her."

"Yeah," Jessica said. "You kind of always are, Darcy."

Darcy put her sandwich down. "You too?" she asked.

"It's true," Jessica said. "But it doesn't matter. I bet if I had a cousin living in a two-family house with me, a nice cousin, I mean, someone my own age, I'd do stuff with her all the time too. It's like having a built-in best friend."

"I thought Darcy and I were best friends," Sara said.

"We are," Darcy said. "And Jessica's my best friend too."

"I knew that," Jessica said. "So have the two of you found books for your book reports yet? I haven't decided what to read, but I guess I'll go to the library this weekend and take something out. My mom likes to go to the library on Saturdays anyway, so I'll tag along and find something then. I wonder if the new Liz Reuben is in."

"It isn't," Darcy said. "I was at the library yesterday, and they didn't have it."

"When were you at the library?" Sara asked.

"Right after I saw you," Darcy replied. "My mom thought it was a good idea for me to get a head start on the book report, the way you were, so I went to the library."

"You could have gone with me," Sara said.

"No I couldn't," Darcy said. "I was at the store while Mom was at the dentist's, remember? Besides, it didn't even occur to me to go until—"

"Until what?" Sara said. "Until you saw me?"

"Right," Darcy said. "Until then."

"I don't believe you," Sara said. "I bet precious April came along and it was her idea, and that's why you went."

"Don't call her that," Darcy said.

"What should I call her then?" Sara asked. "Perfect April? Saint April?"

"She's just my cousin," Darcy said. Her stomach was beginning to hurt. She wondered if she'd ever be able to eat a tuna sandwich again.

"She's more than just your cousin," Sara said. "I have cousins too, three of them, and I never talk about them the way you talk about April."

"Your cousins live in Dallas," Jessica said. "You only see them once a year, and then you don't much like them. Darcy didn't talk about April hardly at all until she moved to West Devon. It's only been since then that she talks about her all the time."

"I think you're both crazy," Darcy said. "I don't talk about April all the time. And I don't think she's perfect. But she does live upstairs from me, and she is my cousin, and we do spend a lot of time together, and I'm sorry I couldn't come over and eat your mother's stupid codfish balls last night, but that had nothing to do with April. You were there, Sara. You know perfectly well it was my mom who said I couldn't go, and that was because I hadn't done my homework and you hadn't given us any advance warning. If you'd told me the day before your mother was going to make stupid codfish balls, then I could have asked my mom the day before, and she could have told me if I got my homework done I could go, and I would have. It's your fault, Sara. It certainly isn't April's."

"Is that what this is all about?" Jessica asked. "Your mother's codfish balls? They're awful. I had them last time and they practically had to pump my stomach."

"I know that," Sara said. "That's why I wanted Darcy to come."

"So I'd get sick?" Darcy asked.

"No," Sara said. "So we could do something together again, the way we used to."

"I never ate your mother's codfish balls," Darcy said.

"You have no idea how lucky you are," Jessica said.

Sara scowled. "I don't just mean codfish balls," she said. "And they aren't as bad as all that, Jessica. It seems to me you managed to eat seconds."

"That was before I knew they were going to make me deathly ill," Jessica replied. "My mother said she'd never seen my face so bright green before."

"Will you leave my mother's codfish balls out of this?" Sara cried. "This is about Darcy, and how she doesn't do stuff with us anymore."

"I do too," Darcy said. "I go to school with you every day, and I have lunch with you, and half the time I see you after school too, and on weekends and everything."

"Not like you used to," Sara said. "Not like last year."

"But last year was different," Darcy said. "Last year was before April moved in."

"But that's my point," Sara said. "You had a lot more time for us before April came."

"You had more time for us before May and June came too," Jessica said. The other girls stared at her. "So it wasn't funny," she said. "I thought a joke might help."

"April doesn't like jokes about her name," Darcy said.

"April isn't here to hear them," Jessica said.

"Darcy'll tell her," Sara said. "Darcy reports home to April about everything. I bet April knows all our secrets, doesn't she, Darcy?"

Darcy blushed. She had told April a secret or two over the past few weeks.

"I don't believe it," Sara said. "You do tell her secrets, don't you?"

"Nothing really serious," Darcy said. "And you tell my secrets all the time, Sara. You told Jessica what I told you about Billy Bowser."

"You told me I could," Sara said.

"But only after you asked," Darcy said. "If you hadn't asked, I wouldn't have let you."

"Why couldn't I know about you and Billy?" Jessica asked. "What's the big deal that he kissed you?"

"Great," Darcy said. "You want to shout it a little louder, Jessica? I don't think they heard you in East Devon."

"I wish Billy Bowser would kiss me," Jessica said, but she said it in a much lower voice.

"I wish April would kiss off," Sara said.

"You take that back," Darcy said.

"Well, I wish she'd leave," Sara said. "Go live with her father wherever it is he lives. Or maybe she could go to boarding school. Rich kids always go to boarding school."

"Not here they don't," Jessica said. "Here, they go to Fairfield."

"April isn't rich," Darcy said. "The only reason she goes to Fairfield is because it offers lots of foreign languages. And I don't know why you don't like her, Sara. She's really nice."

"She's a snob," Sara said. "She never talks to me when I'm over at your place."

"That's because she's shy," Darcy said.

"How shy can she be if she goes around interviewing famous people?" Sara asked. "Shy people don't go on national TV talking about how they met Lyon Fitzhugh all the time."

"She never met him, and she didn't mean to go on national TV," Darcy said. "She talked to him once over the telephone and that was it, and nobody would have cared except his plane went down and she was the last person to talk with him. It isn't her fault she became famous. She isn't famous anymore, except maybe at Fairfield, and I don't think she's even famous there. She's just back to being shy. I wish you'd give her a chance."

"I wish you'd give me a chance," Sara said. "We used to have fun all the time before April moved here."

Darcy stared at her best friend. Sara had stopped

looking mean, and looked kind of sad, instead. "I thought we still spent lots of time together," Darcy said.

"Not like we used to," Sara said. "Last year you and Jessica and I did everything together."

"We did," Jessica said. "Last year was practically the best year of my life, we spent so much time together."

Darcy thought back to last year. She had spent more time with Sara and Jessica then, had more suppers at their houses, invited them over to hers more often. They'd spent practically every weekend together. Lots of times they made videos together, Darcy directing them and Sara and Jessica playing the parts they made up as they went along. But when April moved in, Darcy had felt responsible for her, especially before school started, when April still didn't know anybody. And April hadn't seemed to much like Sara and Jessica. She never said anything bad about them, but she didn't hang out with them or call them up or want them to be her friends. Instead she'd go upstairs, to be by herself, and Darcy would find herself surrounded by her friends, knowing her cousin felt lost and lonely, and that just wasn't right. So she started breaking dates with Sara and Jessica, making videos with April instead, and the next thing she knew, April wasn't just her cousin, she was her best friend, practically her sister, only much better than Isabelle. No wonder Sara and Jessica were mad.

"I'm sorry," she said. "You're right. I do spend more time with April than with you."

"You talk about her all the time too," Sara said.

Darcy wasn't so sure about that, but this was no time to quibble. "Maybe," she said. "I never timed it."

"Does this mean we're best friends again?" Jessica asked.

"We never stopped being best friends," Darcy said. "I just forgot to tell you."

"I have an idea," Sara said. "Let's celebrate. Why don't we have a sleepover Saturday night? Just the three of us. Do you think your mother would mind, Jessica?"

"Why me?" Jessica asked.

"It's quieter at your house," Sara replied. "And we can't have it at Darcy's without inviting April."

Jessica nodded. "Okay," she said. "At my house."

"We could make a Halloween video," Sara said. "Something scary and horrible."

"I want to be the murderer," Jessica said. "You always make me play the corpse."

"That's because you look so good with blood dripping down your face," Sara said. "But okay, this time you get to kill me. What do you say, Darcy? A sleepover, just like we used to have last year."

"That sounds great," Darcy said, trying to remember what she had planned for the weekend. Ice-cream cake popped into her mind first, and then she remembered. "Oh, no. I can't. I'm busy Saturday night."

"I bet she has a date with April," Sara said.

"I do not," Darcy said. "Well, not exactly. It's these girls she knows. They invited both of us to their house for supper Saturday night, and I already said yes."

"Maybe they could come to my sleepover instead?" Jessica said.

Darcy thought about how truly weird the twins were. "I don't think so," she said. "It's a big deal to them, to have us over. April, I mean. I'm just tagging along because I was invited. But I can't cancel out now. It wouldn't be fair."

"You have a funny definition of fair," Sara said. She gathered her books together, then picked up her tray. "Give me a call, Darcy, if you ever want to be friends again."

"Sara," Darcy pleaded, but Sara'd already gotten up. Jessica shook her head, then followed her, leaving Darcy alone at the table she had just moments before shared with her two best friends.

THREE

Darcy had never ridden in a limo before, and even though she knew she was still supposed to be upset over losing her two best friends, she enjoyed the sensation. In her own family, when they rode together, it was an endless pile of bodies and coats and bags of groceries or library books or video equipment. The twins' limo came with its own chauffeur, who opened the door for both April and Darcy, closed it for them as well, and wished them a pleasant evening as he let them off at the twins' front door.

"What's their last name?" Darcy remembered to ask April as they prepared to ring the bell for entrance to what was definitely a first-class mansion.

"Morrow," April replied. "I never told you that?"

Darcy shook her head.

"Megan and Melissa Morrow," April said. "And Megan is the left-handed one."

Darcy grinned. It was she who'd figured that detail out, and now April was trying to teach it to her. Oh, well. April was probably a little nervous, having dinner for the first time with the twins.

A woman opened the door and announced to Megan and Melissa that April and Darcy were there. Soon the twins popped in. Coats were taken, introductions were made ("This is Mrs. Smith, our new housekeeper, and this is Dower, our butler, and this is Mimi, the maid, and you met Marcel, the chauffeur, and this is Daddy . . ."), and Darcy and April found themselves sitting in a modern-looking living room with lots of beautiful paintings.

"Is that a real van Gogh?" Darcy asked.

"It certainly is," Mr. Morrow said. He was a big man, and bald, but he looked good. Darcy had the feeling his suit had been made just for him. Not that her father wore that many suits, but the ones he did came off the discount rack. "I'm impressed you'd recognize it."

"I saw *Lust for Life*," Darcy replied. "It starred Kirk Douglas, and he played van Gogh in it and painted lots of paintings just like this one."

"Daddy collects great art," Megan declared. "He says as long as he has his art collection, we'll never end up in the poorhouse."

"Not that I purchased them solely as investments," Mr. Morrow said. "I love great art. And I want my daughters to grow up in an environment where they're surrounded by objects of enduring beauty."

Darcy thought about what her own home looked like and tried not to giggle.

"So, April," Mr. Morrow said, facing Darcy. "How is your father doing?"

"I'm Darcy," Darcy said. "It's easy to tell us apart, Mr. Morrow. April's prettier than I am."

"Darcy," April said sharply.

"Well, you are," Darcy said. "April's prettier, and I'm more talented."

"Talent can't always be seen," Mr. Morrow said.

"Then just remember April's prettier," Darcy said. "Also, she has blond hair and I'm a brunette."

"My father's fine," April said. "He's been on the news a lot lately. They've been having wars out in Africa, so he's been traveling around covering them."

"Your father has presence," Mr. Morrow said, this time facing the right girl. "A real magnetic quality. Has he ever expressed any interest in doing a Broadway show?"

"I don't think so," April said. "He pretty much always wanted to be a reporter covering Africa."

"I should speak with him the next time he's in the states," Mr. Morrow said. "Remind me to do that, girls."

"All right, Daddy," the twins said in unison. They'd been sitting on footstools by their father's side, looking up adoringly at him. Darcy felt sorry for them. She never had to look adoringly at her father.

"I'd like to see your rooms," she said. "Can I? Do we have time before supper, I mean."

"Sure," Melissa said, getting up instantly. "Come on, Megan. Let's show April and Darcy our bedrooms."

"Is that all right, Daddy?" Megan asked.

"Just bring them back alive," Mr. Morrow said, and then he laughed, so Darcy figured it was a joke. She laughed too. April just smiled.

Megan grabbed April by the hand, and Melissa took Darcy. They ran up the marble staircase, then headed down an extremely long hallway until they were brought to two bedrooms.

"We share a bathroom," Megan said. "See, here." She took the girls into one of the rooms, and sure enough, it had a bathroom with two doors.

"Daddy says for our thirteenth birthday he'll build us an extra bathroom," Melissa said. "He says teenage girls should never have to share a bathroom."

"I share one with Isabelle," Darcy said. Also with her mother and father, she thought. "But I guess I'm not a teenager yet, so it's still okay."

"Melissa and I don't really need our own bathrooms," Megan said. "But Daddy likes to give us things. He says it's because we don't have a mother."

April nodded, like that made sense to her. Darcy hadn't noticed April being showered with things just because her father lived in Kenya. "Where is your mother?" she asked.

"We don't have a mother," Megan said.

"We used to have a mother," Melissa said. "But we don't anymore."

April shot Darcy a "keep quiet" look. Since they were April's friends, Darcy decided to obey it.

"Your rooms are beautiful," April said. They were, too. Beautiful, and absolutely identical. The girls had matching wallpaper, bedspreads, dolls, desks, photographs, and carpets. Darcy checked the paintings on the walls. They weren't identical, but they were by the same artists, so they looked awfully close.

"Daddy always buys two of everything for us," Megan said. "That way neither of us will think the other one has better."

"Can I see your closets?" Darcy asked.

"Darcy!" April said. Darcy got the feeling she was in for a long evening of "Darcy!"'s from April.

"Sure," Melissa said. "This closet's mine." She opened it up, and Darcy stared into a closet almost as big as her own bedroom, lined with dresses and blouses and skirts and slacks and hundreds of pairs of shoes.

"This closet's mine," Megan said, and she opened an identical door in her room, and showed them its identical contents.

"Wow," Darcy said. Not only did each twin have more clothes than her entire family, and not only were the twins' clothes identical, but they were in the exact same order in each closet. "You're both so tidy."

The twins giggled. "We have maids," Megan said. "They're tidy for us."

"Daddy says we're both terribly sloppy," Melissa said. "But he wants us to have the best, so he hires people to make sure we do."

"Daddy loves us so much," Melissa said. "He buys hundreds of valentines in February, and then he gives them to us all year round."

"Identical ones?" Darcy asked.

The twins nodded.

"Even in July?"

The twins nodded.

"What a dad," Darcy said.

"My father sends me flowers," April said. "Sometimes, I mean. On important occasions. Like the first day of school, and my birthday, and last year when I won an award at school for a story I wrote."

"Daddy doesn't send us flowers because he lives with us," Megan said.

"When he goes away though, if we don't go with him, he sends us flowers every day," Melissa said. "Remember, Megan? Last year, when he went to London for two weeks and we couldn't go with him because we had the flu, he sent us flowers every day. Red roses one day, and pink the next, and white the third, and then orchids, and then mixed bouquets, and then back to roses."

"And then when he came home, he said he'd missed us so much, he got us matching sable coats," Megan said. "He said when we outgrew them, we could always give them away to charity."

"He said lots of poor people would be happy to have sable coats to keep them warm in the winter," Melissa said. "Daddy is a very generous man."

"He's going to be a very hungry one if we don't eat soon," Megan said, checking on the time. "Come on. We'd better go downstairs."

So the cousins followed the twins down the endless hallway and down the marble stairs, through several magnificent rooms, until they landed in what was the single classiest dining room Darcy had ever seen, including all the old movies she'd ever watched. There were flowers and silver and crystal chandeliers and china with tiny painted flowers and windows that overlooked gardens and furniture so regal that only Mr. Morrow looked right sitting down.

"This is the family dining room," Megan said. "When Daddy has lots of really important guests, we eat in the company dining room."

"The girls thought you'd be more comfortable here," Mr. Morrow said.

April nodded.

"Someday I'm going to be a great film director," Darcy declared. "Maybe then I'll have dinner with you in your company dining room."

"Maybe indeed," Mr. Morrow said. He rang a little

bell, and before Darcy could blink, the room was filled with servants carrying trays of food. Everything was so pretty, Darcy half expected the Sugar Plum Fairy to pirouette in.

"Eat hearty, girls," Mr. Morrow said, and Darcy noticed, to her relief, that Mr. Morrow was doing just that. She knew she couldn't match him bite for bite, but she definitely held her own.

During dinner, between the endless courses, the twins and April talked about Fairfield Academy. Mr. Morrow listened, and asked lots of questions. He didn't always seem to know who they were talking about, but he really seemed interested.

"Darcy with the brown hair," Mr. Morrow said after they'd finished dessert (which, indeed, had been brought in on fire). "You haven't talked that much this evening."

April giggled. Mr. Morrow turned around and faced her. April turned bright red.

"I talk all the time at home," Darcy said. "That's why April thought it was funny that I was so quiet here."

April nodded, and slowly turned back to pink.

"Is there any reason why you've been so quiet, then?" Mr. Morrow asked.

"I've been thinking a lot," Darcy admitted.

"About what?" Mr. Morrow asked.

"About being rich," Darcy said. "Real whopping rich, like you are. About what my home is going to look like once I'm a great movie director. I never really thought about that before. It always seemed to me the work was what was important, but now I can see it'd be real nice to own lots of beautiful things and have people to take care of you all the time. I really think I'd like that."

"Wealth is a trap," Mr. Morrow said. "You should never get too dependent on things."

"I'll try to remember that," Darcy said, glancing out at the rose garden.

"We don't have much money," April said. "We have enough, we're not poor or anything, but we're not rich, either. I think Darcy's a little overwhelmed."

"I am not," Darcy said. "I've just decided I want wonderful things when I'm a great movie director. That's all. Paintings and flowers and maybe even shoes. I mean more than two pairs. One red and one black. Mom hates shopping for shoes, so that's pretty much all I ever have at one time."

Mr. Morrow nodded. "Would you like more shoes?" he asked. "You could go shoe shopping with Megan and Melissa one day next week, and buy as many pairs as you'd like. How about that, girls? Does that sound like fun?"

"Yes, Daddy!" the twins said. They even sounded like they meant it.

"No, thank you, Mr. Morrow," April said. "We have enough shoes, really."

"Speak for yourself," Darcy said. "Your mother likes to go shoe shopping."

"Then next time you need shoes, go with Mom," April said sharply.

Darcy grinned. "I guess I can't go shoe shopping with the twins," she said. "How about painting shopping instead? Mom never lets me buy enough van Goghs."

Mr. Morrow laughed. April, who at first looked like she wanted to strangle her cousin, relaxed and smiled as well.

"You can never have enough van Goghs," Mr. Morrow said. "Or friends. That's why I was so delighted when Megan and Melissa invited you both over here for dinner tonight. They don't always do that, you know. Invite their friends over."

"They have lots of friends at school," April said. "They're really very popular."

"I'm glad to hear that," Mr. Morrow said. "My work keeps me so busy, I can't always supervise their social lives as much as I would like."

"Everybody loves them," April said. Darcy wondered if that was true. She'd have to remember to ask April when they were back home.

"Darcy's the most popular girl we know," Megan said. "Whenever we go to visit her or April, she always has lots of friends over."

"I used to," Darcy said. "Not anymore."

"What are you talking about?" April asked.

"Didn't I tell you?" Darcy said, and then she realized

of course she hadn't. There had been no way of telling April about her fight with Sara and Jessica without making April feel bad. So she'd kept it to herself. "It's nothing," she said. "Just something I have to work out."

"Perhaps I could help," Mr. Morrow said.

Darcy almost told him he couldn't buy her friends back, but then she thought about how he had really listened to the dinner conversation, which was occasionally more than her own father did, or her mother for that matter. "My friends are kind of jealous of April," she said. "They say I spend too much time with her, and I don't know what to do about it."

"You have to make your friends feel special again," Mr. Morrow said. "That can be quite a challenge. I know. I deal with many brilliant, temperamental people, and if X thinks I'm favoring Y, he sulks and doesn't put out his best work. You must make all your Xs and all your Ys feel like they're the most important people in the world to you."

"How?" Darcy asked. If it meant buying her friends shoes, she couldn't afford it.

"Spend time with them," Mr. Morrow said. "Do something special for them."

"You could give them a party," Megan suggested.

"Yes!" Melissa said. "A party. And Megan and I could come too."

"So could all our friends from Fairfield," Megan said. "And all your friends from the middle school, and that way we could all meet each other, and we'd all have lots more friends. Oh, Daddy, could we? A real party for everybody?"

"Not here," Darcy said. "I mean, no insult intended, but I don't think my friends would be too comfortable here. A lot of them don't plan on being rich when they grow up. They intimidate easily."

"A party would be fun," April said. "Do you think your parents would agree?"

"I don't see why not," Darcy said. "As long as it isn't too big or anything."

"Give me your parents' phone number," Mr. Morrow said. "I insist on paying for the catering. After all, it was my girls' idea to have this party."

"Catering?" Darcy said, not sure that was a great idea. "I just figured we'd buy a couple of bags of potato chips."

"Whatever," Mr. Morrow said. "Now, how many girls do you think you'll invite?"

"Boys and girls, Daddy," Megan said. "Darcy goes to the middle school, where there are boys."

"Ah, yes," Mr. Morrow said. "Boys and girls. Then you can't have any fewer than twenty. Twenty-four would be more like it. If you want even numbers, we know a few boys, nice families, you could have over as well. I suppose some sort of entertainment is in order. You're too old for clowns these days. How about a rock band? Would there be room in your living room for one, as well as space to dance?"

"There wouldn't be," Melissa said. "We're really better off having the party here."

"No," Darcy said. "No rock bands, no caterers, no twenty-four guests. No boys, either. Just four or five of my friends, and four or five of April's. Including Megan and Melissa, of course. A nice little party." Little indeed. She only hoped her mother would see it as little too.

FOUR

"Tell us everything," Isabelle demanded the next day over pancakes. The two families had gotten into the habit of eating Sunday brunch together. This week they were in April's apartment, and her mother had done the cooking. Six days a week Aunt Joanne cooked only sensible foods, but on Sunday she went hog wild. Sundays were definitely Darcy's favorite day to eat upstairs.

"It was very nice," April said, pouring just a little bit of syrup over her pancakes. Darcy waited until she was finished, took the syrup from her, and poured considerably more.

"Darcy," Isabelle said, "I can see April's in her polite mode this morning. Were they rich as Midas?"

"Richer," Darcy replied, taking a satisfying bite of pancake.

"How much richer is richer?" Isabelle persisted.

"Isabelle," her mother said, "it isn't polite to be that interested in material things."

"Besides, poets never get rich," Aunt Joanne said. "So why should you care?"

"Some poets get rich, don't they, Dad?" Isabelle said.

"Sure," her father said. "The ones that get left fortunes by their rich great-aunts."

"Don't look to my side of the family," her mother said. "Or your father's, either, unless he's been keeping something from me all these years."

"I only wish," Darcy's father said. "All right, girls. Satisfy all our curiosity. Just how rich were they?"

"They owned everything," Darcy declared.

"They didn't own their servants," April said.

"Servants?" Aunt Joanne said. "Plural of servant?"

April nodded. "There was a chauffeur and a cook and a butler and a housekeeper and two maids."

"And a stableboy and a gardener, only we didn't meet them," Darcy said. "And the twins had a nanny, only she quit so they got the housekeeper instead. I liked the chauffeur the best. I'm definitely going to have one of those when I'm a great film director."

"They owned all these paintings," April said. "Van Goghs and Monets and Matisses."

"And an itty-bitty Rembrandt," Darcy said. "That's what Megan called it, their itty-bitty Rembrandt. It was kind of small."

"At least compared to their Picasso," April said. "Their Picasso was absolutely huge."

"They're making all this up," Darcy's father declared. "Admit it, girls. This is something the two of you cooked up last night."

"No, Uncle Bill," April said. "It's all true. And they have five cars and a swimming pool and tennis courts and a private gym, and last year when the twins were too sick to go to London, their father gave them matching sable coats."

Aunt Joanne turned pale green. "I may have to rethink Fairfield Academy," she said. "I don't want April to grow up with the wrong kind of values."

"Don't worry about it, Mom," April said. "I could never afford those kinds of values."

Everybody laughed. Darcy slipped herself some extra pancakes while no one was watching.

"Did their father seem nice?" Darcy's mother asked. "Or was he just the kind of guy who throws money around?"

"He was real nice," Darcy said. "Wasn't he, April?"

April nodded. "He really loves the twins," she said. "And they really love him, too."

"Where's their mother?" Isabelle asked.

"We don't know," April replied. "They just said they didn't have one anymore."

"They probably traded her in for an itty-bitty Rembrandt," Darcy's father said.

"Bill!" Darcy's mother said.

"Sorry," he said. "This conversation is just a little rich for my blood first thing in the morning."

"It's eleven," Aunt Joanne said. "And I need to know what kind of friends April's making. Did you feel uncomfortable there, honey? You know, jealous, or left out because they have so much more money than you?"

April shook her head.

"What about you, Darcy?" Darcy's mother asked. "Were you uncomfortable?"

"Absolutely not," Darcy replied. "I felt bad for the twins because they didn't have a mother anymore, and I kind of guessed April was lying when she said everybody at school loved them . . ."

"I wasn't lying," April said. "I just exaggerated a little."

"But I wasn't jealous because they were so rich," Darcy said. "First of all, I'm going to be real rich someday myself. And then I'll support everybody, so we'll all be rich, and then I'll give away all my money to humanitarian causes, so I won't be so rich anymore, but I'll be universally loved, and that's good too."

"I feel better already," her father said. "Be sure to give me the itty-bitty Rembrandt."

"Okay," Darcy said.

"You can't be jealous of people who are that rich," April said. "That's like being jealous of the Grand Canyon. The people you get jealous of are the ones with just a little bit more than you."

"I never thought you were jealous of anybody," Darcy said.

"Sure I am, sometimes," April said. "I used to be jealous of all the friends you had."

"I didn't know that," Darcy said.

"I didn't want you to know," April replied.

"That reminds me," Darcy said. "At supper last night—well, I guess it was more like dinner than supper."

"It was more like a feast than dinner," April said. "I never thought I'd want to eat again, once I was through, but those pancakes are so good, Mom."

"Help yourself," her mother said. "It's Sunday."

"Anyway, we were talking about having a party," Darcy said. "It just sort of came up—what a nice idea it would be if we had a party."

"Who's we?" her mother asked.

"The twins and us," Darcy said. "And we could invite some of my friends and some of April's, so they'd have a chance to meet."

Isabelle burst out laughing.

"What's so funny?" Darcy asked.

"I'm sorry," she said. "It's just the image of Darcy's friends meeting girls with sable coats."

"The twins won't wear their coats," April said. "And my friends aren't any different from Darcy's."

Even Darcy looked at her skeptically.

"Okay, the twins are different," April said. "But they're different from everybody at Fairfield, too."

"You should see their closets," Darcy said. "They have thousands of everything, and they're all identical."

"I can't wait to meet these girls," Darcy's father declared. "They really dress identically?"

"All the time," April said.

"They must have each had a hundred pairs of shoes," Darcy said. "I tried to count, but I lost track after seventy-two."

"Pairs or shoes?" Isabelle asked.

"Pairs," Darcy said. "And their father is so nice. He actually offered . . ." She would have continued, but she could see April shaking her head.

"What did he offer?" Darcy's mother asked.

"Nothing," Darcy said. "Well, he said that when the twins outgrew their sable coats, they could give them to charity, because there are a lot of poor people who'd be happy to have sable coats, so I guess he offered to give away all those shoes, too, once the twins outgrow them."

"He sounds like a very generous man," Darcy's father said. "Tell him you know a poor family that would just love to own its own Rembrandt."

"Really, Dad, you'd prefer the Picasso," Darcy said. "It's a lot bigger."

"I think what Darcy was starting to say was Mr. Morrow was very generous about the party," April said.

"Who's Mr. Morrow?" Isabelle asked.

"That's the twins' father," Darcy said.

"Oh," Isabelle said. "Somehow I never thought he had a name."

"You can miss yesterday, and you can miss today,

[43]

but it's awfully hard to Mister Morrow," Darcy's father said.

"Is it out of your system?" Darcy's mother asked. "Or are you going to keep making jokes like that?"

"I think that's the only one," he replied. "I'll let you know if I feel an attack coming on."

"How was he generous about the party?" Aunt Joanne asked.

"You tell them, April," Darcy said.

April took another bite of pancake. "He just was," she said. "I mean, once we started talking about having a party, he wanted to help."

"How?" Darcy's mother asked. "Was he going have his cook do all the work, or the butler?"

"Neither," Darcy said. "He offered to pay for the catering, instead."

"Catering?" Darcy's father yelped.

"We told him we wouldn't have the party catered," April said. "You don't have to worry, Uncle Bill."

"Who was worried?" Darcy's father said. "We didn't even have our wedding catered. Why should I worry that my twelve-year-old daughter's party is going to be?"

"Our wedding was catered," Darcy's mother said.

"You told me you did all the cooking yourself," he said. "You and Joanne and your mother. You mean you lied all these years?"

Darcy's mother nodded.

"Nobody in their right mind cooks for their own

wedding, Bill," Aunt Joanne said. "We were sure you knew we were joking."

"I swear I thought you did all the cooking," Darcy's father said. "The roast beef was overcooked, just the way your mother always makes it."

"This is neither the time nor the place to criticize my mother's cooking," Darcy's mother said. "What else did Mr. Morrow offer to do?"

"Not much," April said.

"Just the rock band," Darcy said.

"Rock band?" Isabelle asked. "Anybody famous?"

"I don't know," April said. "Darcy said no to that."

"I thought you wanted me to," Darcy said.

"I liked the idea of a rock band," April said. "At least I'd have liked to know who he was going to hire."

"I don't believe you," Darcy said. "You wouldn't let me go shoe shopping with the twins, and now you're complaining because I said no to the rock band."

"Shoe shopping?" Darcy's mother asked.

"Darcy was going on and on about how she doesn't have any shoes," April said. "So naturally Mr. Morrow offered to let her go shoe shopping with the twins. He really is the nicest man. Only Darcy has enough shoes, so I said she didn't have to go."

"I don't have enough shoes," Isabelle declared. "Could I go instead?"

"Are you sure you want to keep sending April to Fairfield?" Darcy's mother asked Aunt Joanne.

Aunt Joanne shook her head. "It wasn't my idea,"

she said. "It was Mitch's. He said it was important April learn as many languages as possible, and Fairfield had the best language department around here."

"I like Fairfield," April said. "I have friends there now. Do I have to leave just because the twins are so rich?"

"Of course not," her mother said. "Just as long as we all remember nobody's taking us shoe shopping."

"Drat," Isabelle said. "I bet I'm too big for their hand-me-down sables."

"I'm sorry," Darcy said to April. "It never occurred to me you wanted the rock band."

"I knew it wouldn't fit here," April said. "It was just kind of a dream."

"Here?" Aunt Joanne said. "You mean in this apartment, here?"

April nodded. "Or in Darcy's," she said. "There'd be even less space there for a rock band."

"We're giving this party?" Aunt Joanne asked.

"Sure," Darcy said. "I thought you knew."

"Why else would Mr. Morrow offer to cater it?" Isabelle asked. "Even I figured that much out."

"I'm slow on Sundays," Aunt Joanne declared. "You and Darcy and the twins and Mr. Morrow all decided to throw a party here, in my home, without asking my permission first. Is that what you're telling us?"

April bit hard on her lower lip. Darcy stared around the kitchen. April was the first to nod.

"So can we?" Darcy asked. "Have the party, I mean.

It won't be catered, and we won't have a rock band. Just some friends. The twins offered to have it at their house, but we didn't think that was such a good idea, so we said no, we'd have it here."

"Why can't the twins have it at their house?" Isabelle asked. "I'd go if it was held there."

"Because the party's as much for my friends as it is for April's," Darcy said. It seemed to her the party was supposed to be more for her friends, but she didn't care to explain that to her family just then. "And my friends wouldn't know how to act in a house with Picassos."

"I'm not sure I would," her father said. "But I don't see what the fuss is. Why can't Darcy and April have a little party here? Uncatered, the same as our wedding."

"How little is little?" Aunt Joanne asked.

"Not big at all, Mom," April said. "Maybe twelve girls? Darcy and five of her friends and me and five of mine. That's counting the twins as two."

"We'll do all the cleaning up ourselves," Darcy said. "And preparing, too. Mom, you were saying just the other day what a good idea it would be for my friends and April's to get to know each other."

"You never told me that," Aunt Joanne said.

"I meant to," Darcy's mother said. "And it is a good idea. Or at least I thought it was when I thought all twelve-year-old girls were basically the same. That was before dinner last night."

"The twins won't wear their sables," April said. "No

one will even know who's rich and who isn't. Please, Mom?"

"Please, Mom?" Darcy said.

Darcy's mother and Aunt Joanne exchanged looks.

"It'll be simple," Aunt Joanne said. "And you'll do all the preparing and straightening up afterward?"

"Promise," April said.

"Twelve girls, no boys," Darcy's mother said.

"Promise," Darcy said.

The cousins' mothers nodded. "All right," Aunt Joanne said. "Maybe it is a good idea, after all."

"Thank you!" Darcy cried. "It's going to be the best party ever."

Everybody stared at her.

"Well, the best uncatered un-rock-band party ever," she said, and then they all laughed and finished off the pancakes.

FIVE

Darcy thought about calling Sara and Jessica on Sunday to tell them about the party, but she wasn't sure if they were having a sleepover, or even if they'd take a phone call from her. It was easier, and more fun, to spend the day with April, making plans. And then there was homework to do, and stuff to watch on TV, and before she knew it, it was time for bed.

So by the time lunch came around on Monday, Darcy was impatient to speak to Sara and Jessica. She found the two of them sitting by themselves in the lunchroom and grabbed a chair next to theirs.

"I don't remember inviting anyone to join us," Sara said. "Do you, Jessica?"

"No," Jessica said, but she looked uncomfortable. Sara just looked mean.

"Oh, stop it," Darcy said. "I'm sorry, I apologize,

you're my best friends now and for always. Besides, there's something I want to talk to you about."

"Sure," Sara said. "When it's something you want to talk about, there's time for us."

Darcy raised her eyes to the heavens. "How much more apologizing do you want?" she asked.

"A little more," Jessica said.

"A lot more," Sara said.

Darcy grinned. "I'll start with Jessica then," she said. "I really am sorry, Jessica. You were right. I have been spending an awful lot of time with April, and time with her friends, too, and that means I haven't had enough time for you. I miss you, and I miss doing stuff with you, and April is more settled in her school now and has her own friends, so could we please make up, because I'd love to do stuff with you again, like we used to. Please?"

Jessica nodded. "I'd like that," she said. "I didn't like being mad at you all weekend."

"I'm madder than Jessica," Sara declared. "And I'm not at all ready to forgive you yet."

Darcy shrugged her shoulders. "Okay," she said. "Then I'll just talk to Jessica."

"Jessica," Sara said.

"Stop it," Jessica said. "I'm not about to pick between the two of you, especially when you know, Sara, that you'll make up with Darcy sooner or later."

"Sooner, I hope," Darcy said.

"All right," Sara said. "Talk with Darcy. But don't expect me to talk too."

Darcy tried not to giggle. Sara could never keep from talking. But she made sure to face Jessica and talk directly to her.

"I had an idea this weekend," she said. "Well, I'm not sure it was really my idea, but it's a good one anyway, and that's to have a party."

"A party?" Jessica asked. "What kind of a party?"

"All girls," Darcy said. "The idea is, half the guests'll be my friends, and half will be April's. Since April goes to an all-girls school, she doesn't know any boys, so if I had to invite boys, I wouldn't be able to invite any girls, and that would be dumb, since most of the reason why I'm giving the party is so you and Sara won't be mad at me anymore."

"If you gave a party and only invited boys and didn't invite me, I'd be real mad," Jessica said. "As mad as Sara."

"That's what I figured," Darcy said. "And I have to invite April and her friends because it was kind of her friends' idea that we have this party. Those girls we had dinner with Saturday night. They're twins, and it was their idea to have the party, so they had to be invited too. We figure twelve girls, including April and me. And you just have to come, Jessica. I won't have any fun at all if you're not there."

"What about Sara?" Jessica asked.

"She has to come too," Darcy said, as though Sara weren't two feet away. "The two of you have been my best friends for so long, I could never have fun at a party without you. And the reason for the party is to make you feel special. It's like the party's for you and Sara. April doesn't have to make her friends feel special, because she hasn't had them for so long." She took a bite out of her macaroni and cheese and waited for Sara to forgive her.

"When's the party?" Jessica asked.

"Sunday afternoon," Darcy said.

"If Sara and I come, who else will you invite?" Jessica asked.

"I wanted your advice on that," Darcy said. "I'd like to ask Jen and Donna, but I'm not sure they're still talking to each other."

"They're not," Jessica replied. "Not since Jen said Donna stole two dollars from her."

"Should I invite one of them but not the other?" Darcy asked. "Or should I invite both of them and hope they make up, or should I not invite either of them?"

"If you don't invite either of them, who else would you ask?" Jessica asked. "Michelle?"

"I was going to ask her, no matter what," Darcy said. "And I thought I'd ask Marie, if I didn't ask Jen or Donna. She's new, but she seems real nice, and I don't think she's made many friends yet. What do you think?"

"I like Marie," Jessica said. "Michelle was thinking

about inviting her over someday, so your party might be a nice way for us to know her better."

Darcy smiled. "So the list is you and Michelle and Marie definitely, and maybe Jen and Donna."

"What about me?" Sara asked. "I thought I was invited."

"Of course you are," Darcy said. "I just didn't know if you'd come."

"I don't know that I will," Sara said. "It sounds like most of the guests are going to be April's rich friends."

"I guess they are rich," Darcy said. "But they're really nice. And the twins. Well, they might be rich, but they're strange, so you're so busy noticing that, you don't even realize how rich they are. And none of them are snobs."

"I've met girls from Fairfield," Sara said. "And they all seemed like snobs to me."

"Good," Darcy said. "Then you can come to the party, and if they still seem like snobs to you, you'll know you're right. Isabelle loves being right about things. She says it's more fun than being wrong, even if it's sometimes better to be wrong than to be right, if you know what I mean."

"If I think they're snobs, can I say so?" Sara asked.

"Sure," Darcy said. "Why not?"

"I mean right to their faces," Sara said. "Can I walk up to one of them and call her a snob right at your party?"

Darcy took another bite of macaroni and cheese, to

give herself a chance to think that one over. She'd met all the girls April was planning on asking, and they'd all seemed perfectly nice to her. If Sara was determined to think they were snobs, then she would, but it wouldn't be because of anything April's friends did. Then again, if Sara was only agreeing to come to the party to make a scene and embarrass Darcy, who needed her?

"No," Darcy said. "You can't be rude to them. Not at my party."

"Why not?" Sara asked. "Because you like them more than you like me?"

"Because I wouldn't let them be rude to you, either," Darcy said. "Think about it, Sara. My parents are going to be at this party. My big sister probably will be. My cousin certainly will, and my aunt, too, and if you go around calling half the guests snobs, whether they are or not, I'm the one who's going to have to live with it for the next twenty years of my life, if not more. Forget it. You want to call them snobs, write them anonymous notes. Or sign the notes for all I care, just as long as you do it away from my house."

"She has a point," Jessica said. "I think you're being stupid, Sara."

"I could invite Alexa," Darcy said. "She wouldn't think they're snobs, because she doesn't know what snob means."

"No," Jessica said. "It has four letters, and she hasn't learned more than three yet."

Darcy and Jessica giggled. Sara didn't, but at least she didn't scowl.

"I think you should invite Kristen," Jessica said. "If you don't invite Jen or Donna. And if Sara comes."

"Kristen," Darcy said. "That's a good idea. She gets along with everybody."

"And she told me the other day how nice Marie is," Jessica said. "So let's see. It's Michelle and Marie and Kristen and me and Jen or Donna or Sara." She smiled at Darcy.

"Sara's my first choice," Darcy said. "If she agrees to behave herself." She ate some more of the macaroni and cheese. It tasted like canned paste.

"Would you really do that?" Sara asked. "Have a party and refuse to let me come unless I practically sign a piece of paper swearing I won't open my mouth the entire time I'm there?"

"Sara," Darcy said. "I want you to open your mouth. I just don't want you to put your foot in it while it's open."

Jessica giggled. Sara glared at her.

"Come on," Jessica said. "You called me up five times this weekend to complain that Darcy wasn't spending enough time with us, that she didn't like us anymore, that all she wanted to do was hang out with those rich girls from Fairfield. And now she's throwing us a party, and you're not even acting like you like the idea. You know you want to go. And you know you'll behave yourself, and not say anything obnoxious, because you're a very nice person, Sara, and smart, and the last thing in the world you'd want to do is make a fool of yourself like that. And Darcy didn't ask you to sign anything, and you know it."

"I don't know," Sara said. "I heard Darcy apologize to you for hours practically and she hasn't apologized to me, and maybe she doesn't really want to be friends with me anymore."

"Of course I do," Darcy said. "I even want to eat your mother's codfish balls."

"No you don't," Jessica said. "Believe me."

"They can't be worse than this macaroni and cheese," Darcy said.

"They're a close second," Jessica declared. "So what are you going to do, Sara? Sulk for the rest of your life, or admit you want to be friends with Darcy and agree to go to the party, and have a good time?"

"Are those my only choices?" Sara asked, and for the first time in days she sounded like Sara.

" 'Fraid so," Darcy said. "Sara, I really am sorry. I hate the idea that you're mad at me because of something I've done. You're my best friend ever, you and Jessica, and I wouldn't know what to do if you weren't my friend. Well, I'd know what to do. I'd cry and be miserable, but that isn't any fun, and you are, so please be my friend again." She gave Sara what her father called her killer look. It had gotten her most of what she'd wanted in life, except a pony and a trip to Disney World.

"Are you all right?" Sara asked. "You look like you're sick or something."

"It's the macaroni and cheese," Darcy said. She guessed the look only worked with fathers. Drat. "So, are you going to forgive me?"

"I forgive you," Sara said. "But mostly so I can go to this party and see what the twins look like."

"They're identical," Darcy said. "Except Megan's right-handed and Melissa's left-handed. But what's really weird about them is they dress identically. They're kind of nice though, once you get used to them."

"April's nice too," Jessica said. "I've been meaning to tell you that."

Darcy nodded. "She is nice," she said. "She's a little bit shy, though. But I'm really hoping her friends and mine will like each other. I don't see how her friends couldn't like mine, and I know April feels the same way about hers, so it should be okay."

"I put a curse on you this weekend," Sara said. "Kind of a voodoo curse, only I made it up. I don't suppose you were sick or anything over the weekend?" She looked just a little bit hopeful.

Darcy shook her head. "I'm afraid not," she said. "But this macaroni and cheese is making me sick. I can't eat any more of it and live."

"You never know with curses," Jessica said. "I once put one on my big brother, and sure enough he got sick, and I felt terrible. I mean, I didn't really want him to get sick if it was going to be my fault, only it turned out he was allergic to strawberries and that's what made him sick. And he'd put a curse on me at the exact same time, and nothing happened to me because I'm not allergic to strawberries. I'm allergic to carrots, but I don't like them anyway, so what do I care, but my brother likes strawberries, so even though he's allergic, he eats them, and that's why it wasn't my fault when I put the curse on him."

"I'm glad my curse didn't work," Sara said. "Although I kind of wish it had, because it would be great knowing you really could make people sick, just a little bit, I mean, and then if you wanted them to be, you could just put the curse on them."

"I think I'd rather be rich," Darcy said, "than be able to put curses on people."

"Are you really through with lunch?" Sara asked.

Darcy nodded. "Why?" she asked. "Do you want to finish it for me?"

"No thank you," Sara said. "It's just my mother baked yesterday, oatmeal cookies and brownies and all kinds of good stuff like that, and she froze most of it, but not all, so if you're still hungry after school because you didn't eat much lunch, you could come over to my house and we could pig out."

"That sounds wonderful," Darcy said. "I'd love to."

"What about you, Jessica?" Sara asked. "Mom baked carrot cake, but we'd make sure you didn't eat any of it."

"I'd like to," Jessica said. "But I haven't even started

reading the book for the book report yet, and that's due on Friday."

"I wrote my report over the weekend," Sara said. "After I finished putting the curse on Darcy."

Darcy remembered that she hadn't even looked at the book April had made her take out. She knew she should go home and begin reading it. But there was still practically a whole week until Friday, and she didn't dare break a date with Sara. "I'll eat Jessica's share," she said. "Thanks for asking me, Sara. It sounds like fun."

SIX

Darcy stared out the schoolroom window and felt very pleased with life. The party idea had accomplished everything she'd hoped for. She'd gone over the day before to Sara's house, devoured her mother's cookies, called Kristen, Marie, and Michelle to invite them to the party (and they'd all accepted), and ended up staying at Sara's for supper. Of course, she'd had to tell her mother that she'd already done her homework, which was kind of not true, but Darcy knew she'd do what she had to that night when she got home, and she had. A little math, a little science, a long conversation with April, who reported that all her friends had accepted their invitations as well, and then it was time for bed. Definitely one of the best days of her life.

"Please pass the papers back," Ms. Slocum, the social-studies teacher, said.

What papers? Darcy, who was second in her row,

found herself passing something back before she even had a chance to see what it was that had been given to her.

"This test shouldn't take more than twenty minutes to complete," Ms. Slocum declared. "The first section is worth sixty points. Each correct answer in the second section is worth four points, for a total of forty. There are no trick questions. If you've been keeping up with your work and studied yesterday, you should have no problems."

Studied for what? Darcy felt like she was in the middle of a bad dream.

Everybody else seemed to know what was going on. Darcy looked around, hoping to see another kid with the same panicked look she knew she had, but they were all looking down at their papers, biting on their pens and pencils, ready for action. Darcy looked at her paper. It was definitely a test, and it was equally definitely on state capitals. That's what they'd been studying all right, state capitals. Darcy closed her eyes for a moment and concentrated. Ms. Slocum had mentioned something last week about how they'd be tested on their capitals. And she must have said the test would be on Tuesday. But Darcy had had other things on her mind Friday, like losing her two best friends, and she'd spent the weekend coming up with ways of getting them to be her friends again, and then yesterday she'd spent being friends, and she'd totally forgotten about the test. She certainly hadn't studied for it. She'd even been grateful the night before that she hadn't had any social-studies homework to do. Now she knew why. She was supposed to be memorizing her state capitals.

Darcy told herself not to panic. She liked geography, learning where places belonged, and what each city or country was like. She knew when she was a great film director she would travel all over the world. She'd shoot her movies on location in Saudi Arabia and China and Albania and lots of other countries that ended in *a*, places no one she knew had ever been to. She liked learning about the states as well, since she could better imagine all the people who lived in California and North Dakota and Michigan going to see her movies when she knew where those states were and how many people lived in them. She'd always paid attention during class and kept up with her homework. Until last Friday, that is. And now a test was staring her in the face, and she knew she didn't have the slightest idea what the capital of North Dakota was.

Darcy couldn't remember ever taking a test she hadn't studied for. She'd always done well in school, because she'd studied and done her homework and cared about her grades. She looked at the clock. Two minutes had already gone by, and she hadn't even read the test paper yet. Everybody else was working on theirs, and she still didn't know what the questions were. She felt her heart beating faster.

She swallowed hard and forced herself to concentrate on the paper. The first part consisted of two columns.

One was names of states, the other was names of cities. She was to match them, capital to state. There were twenty states, twenty cities. None of them looked familiar. She didn't dare look at the second part of the test.

What if she handed in the paper completely blank? She could claim she'd gotten amnesia and had forgotten everything she'd ever known. That even felt like it was true. But Ms. Slocum didn't seem like the kind of teacher who'd buy the amnesia explanation. Darcy choked back a wild giggle. Twenty states, twenty state capitals. She had to know one or two of them. Just putting something down on the paper would make the rest of the test seem easier.

Oklahoma. Oklahoma City. They had to go together. Ms. Slocum had said there were no tricks.

But wasn't Kansas City in Missouri? Darcy stared at the list. Kansas was on the state list, and Kansas City wasn't, which must mean Kansas City was the capital of Missouri and not Kansas, and in that case Oklahoma City could be the capital of just about anywhere except maybe France or England, only they weren't states so they weren't on the test. It wasn't fair. Darcy knew their capitals—Paris and London—cities April had been to and Darcy had dreamed of seeing. She never wanted to see Oklahoma City, especially if it wasn't in Oklahoma. If Kansas City was in Missouri, then Oklahoma City could well be the capital of Kansas. It made sense to Darcy. When she couldn't have something Isabelle had (a big closet), she tried to get something April had (a new desk). Oklahoma City was Kansas's new desk.

But didn't that make it a trick question? And Ms. Slocum had said there were no trick questions.

But Ms. Slocum was a teacher, and what seemed fair to teachers might not seem fair to the rest of the world. It was no trick question if you knew about Kansas and Missouri, which was practically the only thing Darcy was sure she did know. So she marked down that the capital of Kansas was Oklahoma City, and regretted only that Missouri wasn't on the list, so she could put down Kansas City as its capital.

Hawaii. Honolulu. That Darcy was confident of. Two down, eighteen to go. She was already breathing a little less rapidly.

Denver, Colorado. She knew that from football. Her father always bet with his friends on the Denver Broncos, and once her mother said if her father had just not bet and saved all that money they could afford a trip to Colorado where they could see the Denver Broncos lose in person. That meant two she was sure of, and one probable, and only seventeen left.

Darcy stared at the unmarked states and cities, trying to find pairings that felt right to her. But they were just names, endless names, meaningless, ridiculous, stupid names. Who cared what the capital of Washington was?

Wait a second. There was Helena on the list. And Washington was the place with the volcano, and that was Mt. Saint Helens, so its capital had to be Helena. Darcy allowed herself a smile. This wasn't so hard once you got the hang of it.

Bismarck. Hadn't there been someone important named Bismarck in German history? Darcy was almost positive Isabelle had mentioned something about Bismarck when she'd studied world history the year before. That meant Darcy had to find a state that sounded kind of German, and attach Bismarck to it. She read the list. Oregon. That sounded German, so Bismarck must belong there.

Salem. That was easy. The Salem witch trials happened in Massachusetts. When April had lived in Massachusetts, Darcy's family had gone to visit her, and they'd even gone to Salem. Of course that meant Boston wasn't the capital of Massachusetts, but that made sense too, once you thought about it. New York City wasn't the capital of New York, and Los Angeles didn't seem to be the capital of California, because it wasn't on the list anywhere and California was, so why should Boston be the capital of Massachusetts? Of course Boston was on the list, and so was Massachusetts, and that meant Darcy had to find a state for Boston to be capital of, but there were still plenty left. Besides, there were a lot of people from Boston who must have moved out west, looking for gold or something, and they took the name with them and made it their state capital. They probably felt it was unfair Boston wasn't the capital of Massachusetts, so they made it the capital of someplace else.

Which meant one of those west gold-rushy kinds of states. California maybe. They'd had a gold rush, and Darcy's father was always talking about how people from all over the country moved there. If Los Angeles couldn't be the capital of California, it seemed only right Boston should be. Darcy marked it down.

Pierre. That sounded French. But so did Juneau and Baton Rouge. And there was only one state on the list that Darcy knew was French and that was Louisiana. At least New Orleans wasn't on the list, which would really have confused things. One of those French names had to belong to Louisiana. Darcy did eeny-meeny-miney-mo and ended up with Pierre. That sounded the most French anyway, so Darcy figured it was a definite yes.

Of course, that left her with Baton Rouge and Juneau looking for homes and no more French states to put them in. Maine didn't have any capital attached to it, and they had French people there, French Canadians, so Darcy gave them Baton Rouge. Juneau she attached to Alaska because Alaska ended in an *a*, same as Louisiana and Albania.

Darcy looked at the test. She'd already put ten answers down, exactly half. The other ten had to be easy, now that she understood how states got their capitals.

Montgomery. There were movie stars named Montgomery, and that meant it should probably be the capital of California, but the more Darcy looked at her paper, the surer she was Boston belonged there. So Montgomery had nothing to do with movie stars. But wasn't that the last name of the woman who wrote the *Anne of Green Gables* books? They took place in Canada, Darcy knew, but Canada bordered lots of the United States, and if she lived in one of those cold places right next to Canada, she'd probably feel Canadian most of the time. She stared at the list. North Dakota didn't have a capital yet. She gave it Montgomery.

South Dakota. It didn't seem fair to Darcy that she was supposed to know the capitals of both North and South Dakota, but that didn't mean both states weren't entitled to capitals. South Carolina was on the list too. Darcy was relieved to see there were no capitals with South in their names, since she wouldn't have known who to give what to.

Augusta was free. It sounded southern. Darcy put it down as the capital of South Carolina. But what to do about South Dakota? She knew she was running short of time, and the second part of the test still awaited.

Little Rock. Little Rock, South Dakota. There were badlands somewhere around South Dakota, and maybe they were bad because they had lots of little rocks. Darcy's mother loved to garden, and she was always complaining about rocks. That had to be right.

Olympia. Columbia. Topeka. Why did everything have to end with the letter *a*? There weren't that many states left, and Darcy knew she'd gotten most of the answers right, so just by guessing, she was sure she'd do okay. Olympia was Greek, Columbia was Spanish. Darcy wasn't sure what Topeka was, which probably meant it had something to do with Native Americans. They got a lot of names. Darcy looked for a state with a Native American name and no capital, found Arkansas, and matched Topeka to it.

That still left Olympia and Columbia to find states for, but Darcy was beginning to enjoy herself. It was kind of like matchmaking, what capital fit best with what state. Columbia she assigned to Florida, since it had a large Spanish population. Olympia was tougher, since Darcy didn't know any states with lots of Greeks, but she figured it was probably a state with colleges instead, or athletes. Olympia, Olympics—only, Massachusetts and California were both taken.

But Rhode Island wasn't, and Rhode Island was the smallest state in the union. It would want the grandest name. So Darcy marked the two of them together.

There were only four left. Alabama, New Hampshire, Montana, and Oklahoma. Concord, Tallahassee, Providence, and Sacramento. Darcy didn't have the slightest idea which city went with which state, but she was running out of time and she figured she had at least a one in four chance of getting each answer right. Tallahassee she gave to Alabama, because it sounded kind of like Mississippi, and she knew Alabama and Mississippi were right next to each other. The only Concord she knew was in Massachusetts, but that was taken with Salem, so she gave it to New Hampshire, since they were both in New England. Poor old Oklahoma didn't even get to have Oklahoma City as its capital, but Darcy knew Providence was a big city in Rhode Island, so it might as well be the capital of Oklahoma to even things out. That left Sacramento, Montana, and why not?

Darcy couldn't believe it. She'd actually finished the first and most important section of the test. She knew she couldn't count on all sixty points, but she figured she had a fighting chance at forty of them, and that gave her a pretty good shot at actually passing, which was all she could hope for.

She read the second section quickly. There were five states listed. All she had to do was name their capitals (four points each) and explain how each capital had gotten its name (four points each). How hard could that be? After all, twenty capitals were already taken, which meant she could ignore their names.

The states were Missouri, North Carolina, Ohio, Utah, and Wisconsin. Darcy felt panic swell back inside her. She had no idea what those states' capitals were. Why couldn't Ms. Slocum have asked New York (Albany) or Arizona (Phoenix)? Why had she picked five states Darcy had practically never even heard of?

Utah. The capital of Utah was Salt Lake City. Darcy knew that! Her family had gotten a postcard just the summer before from her father's brother and his family, and they sent it from Salt Lake City. Darcy was sure it was the capital, and even if it wasn't, it was the only city she knew in Utah, so she might as well hope for the best.

"The capital of Utah is Salt Lake City, which gets its name from the Great Salt Lake it's near." That was eight points right there.

Missouri. Well, its capital had to be Kansas City. Darcy had based practically all her answers in the first part of the test on that.

"The capital of Missouri is Kansas City, which gets its name from Kansas the state it ought to be in."

Darcy didn't know how to word it any better than that. If Ms. Slocum wanted to know how Kansas got its name, she was asking the wrong person.

Ohio. The big city there was Cleveland, and there was definitely a President Cleveland.

"The capital of Ohio is Cleveland and it gets its name from President Cleveland." Another eight points she could count on.

North Carolina. Darcy looked at the top of the test paper to see what the capital of South Carolina had turned out to be. Augusta. No help there. Wait a second. They grew tobacco in North Carolina, so their state capital probably sounded like a cigarette. And there was a city called Winston-Salem in North Carolina. She remembered that from two weeks ago, because it had been so funny there was an entire city named for cigarettes.

"The capital of North Carolina is Winston-Salem and

it gets its name from cigarettes because that's what they make in North Carolina." That had to be right.

Wisconsin. Darcy had no idea what the capital of Wisconsin might be. She was no longer sure she remembered where Wisconsin was. She could leave it blank; it would be the only unanswered question on the test. But there was always the off chance a guess might prove right, and she knew she could use as many points as she could get.

There should be at least one state with a capital named for George Washington, she decided. Of course there was Washington State and Washington, D.C., but even so. Everybody liked George Washington.

"The capital of Wisconsin is Washington City, and it got its name from George Washington our first president."

"Time's up! Please pass your papers forward."

Darcy handed her paper in with a sigh of relief. She never wanted to think about state capitals again.

"Anything interesting happen in school today?" her mother asked her that night at supper.

"We had kind of a surprise quiz in social studies," Darcy replied, helping herself to the chicken curry. "I had to guess at some of the answers, but I used logic, so I think I did okay."

SEVEN

20.

Darcy stared at her test paper. She'd never seen a twenty written on a test before. She supposed other people, when they got twenties, didn't pass them around, so the only way she could see one would be if it was on one of hers. Which this twenty was.

She was still in a state of shock when the bell rang and all the kids got up to go to their next classes. But Ms. Slocum had asked her to stay behind. Darcy was just as happy not to join her friends, who were comparing their test scores merrily. It seemed to have been a pretty easy test if you knew all the answers.

"Darcy, come over here," Ms. Slocum said, gesturing for Darcy to take a front seat. Darcy was relieved to see Ms. Slocum didn't seem angry. Teachers, she supposed, got angry at fifty-sevens and sixty-twos, but twenties must be regarded like earthquakes and floods.

Natural disasters you just helped survivors from and didn't blame anyone for.

"I got a twenty," Darcy said, just in case Ms. Slocum had forgotten and thought she'd gotten a sixteen or a twelve.

"I know," Ms. Slocum said. "I marked the paper myself."

Darcy nodded. Ms. Slocum had probably stayed up half the night marking their social-studies tests. She'd probably gone over Darcy's two or three times. Maybe she was just too tired to scream.

"Darcy, you're a bright girl," Ms. Slocum said. "Your grades have been very good up until now."

Darcy looked down at the floor.

Ms. Slocum smiled at her. "Sometimes things upset us in life," she said. "And they make it hard for us to concentrate on our schoolwork."

Darcy nodded. "I know what you mean," she said, glad that Ms. Slocum understood the potential loss of two best friends and having to arrange for a party made it nearly impossible to concentrate on anything.

"Are there problems at home?" Ms. Slocum asked. "Are your parents fighting a lot, or maybe talking about a divorce? That could be very upsetting to a girl your age."

Darcy shook her head. Her parents hugged and kissed a lot more often than they fought.

"That's good," Ms. Slocum said. "But there still could be other problems, other concerns. Maybe your parents are worried about money. I know they own a business. Is it doing well?"

"Sure," Darcy said. "We might even go to Disney World during winter vacation."

"Grandparents, then," Ms. Slocum said. "Are they worried about your grandparents? Is there any talk that one of them might move in with you, might even share your room?"

"No," Darcy said.

Ms. Slocum looked even more serious. "How's Isabelle?" she asked. "I remember her from when she took social studies with me."

"She's okay," Darcy said.

"She must be about sixteen now," Ms. Slocum said. "That's such a difficult age these days."

"She's difficult, all right," Darcy said, glad she had finally found something Ms. Slocum really understood.

"In what way?" Ms. Slocum asked.

"Well, you know," Darcy said, finding it hard to pinpoint exactly what was difficult about Isabelle. "She writes poetry all the time, so she's always telling me to be quiet. She likes her privacy."

"Sometimes girls that age, or poets any age— sometimes they do things they shouldn't," Ms. Slocum said. "Drink, or even take drugs. Do you suppose Isabelle ever does that?"

"No," Darcy said. "I would know if she did."

"How?" Ms. Slocum asked. "How would you know?"

"We practically share a bedroom," Darcy replied. "Dad put up a partition, but it's real thin. That's why she wants me to be quiet all the time."

Ms. Slocum nodded. "Darcy, has anybody ever offered you drugs?" she asked. "Or given you something alcoholic to drink, like beer?"

"No," Darcy said. "That stuff's really bad for you. I wouldn't do anything like that."

"I want to make sure I have this straight," Ms. Slocum said. "Your parents aren't quarreling, aren't talking about a divorce, aren't worried about their parents or money. Isabelle doesn't drink or take drugs, neither do you. Is that right?"

"Right," Darcy said.

"Then why in heaven's name did you think Oklahoma City was the capital of Kansas?" Ms. Slocum cried.

"Because Kansas City is the capital of Missouri," Darcy said.

"No it isn't," Ms. Slocum said.

"You mean I got that one wrong too?" Darcy asked. She scanned her paper, and sure enough, there were two Xs next to the capital-of-Missouri question.

"Darcy, you got a twenty on the test," Ms. Slocum said. "I think you should work on the assumption you got everything wrong."

"Kansas City is in Missouri, isn't it?" she asked.

"Yes, it is," Ms. Slocum said. "But that's no reason to make Oklahoma City the capital of Kansas. I've been teaching social studies for ten years, and you are the first student I've ever had who got that question wrong. It's like who's buried in Grant's Tomb, Darcy. It just stands to reason that Oklahoma City is the capital of Oklahoma."

"Then why isn't Kansas City the capital of Kansas?" Darcy asked.

"Because Topeka is the capital," Ms. Slocum replied. "Not the capital of Arkansas. Is that how you got confused? Kansas, Arkansas?" She deliberately mispronounced Arkansas so it sounded like Kansas.

"No," Darcy said. "I never even thought about how they were almost the same state."

Ms. Slocum sighed. "Darcy, you're a smart enough girl to know Boston is the capital of Massachusetts, not California," she declared. "You're the only student who got that one wrong."

"I kind of wondered why it was in California," Darcy admitted. "But I figured if Los Angeles wasn't the capital of California, then why shouldn't Boston be? If you know what I mean."

"I don't," Ms. Slocum said. "And I don't have the energy left to hear your explanation."

"I'm sorry," Darcy said.

"What surprises me is the questions you got correct," Ms. Slocum said. "All right, Denver, Colorado, is pretty easy, although not based on your logic. But you knew Juneau was the capital of Alaska, and most of the other kids got that one wrong."

"That's because it sounded French," Darcy said, glad to teach Ms. Slocum a system. "And Alaska ends in an *a*, just like Louisiana."

Ms. Slocum massaged her forehead.

"I tried really hard with the test," Darcy said, looking at her paper, shocked at how many states didn't have the capitals she'd assigned to them. "Florida has a lot of Spanish people, so I gave them Columbia. And Montgomery belonged in North Dakota because of *Anne of Green Gables*."

"I almost gave you two points for Cleveland and for Winston-Salem," Ms. Slocum said. "At least they're in the states you assigned them to. But even with the four extra points, you would have only gotten a twenty-four."

"That wouldn't have helped much," Darcy said.

"No," Ms. Slocum said. "That wouldn't have helped much."

"I guess you think I didn't study," Darcy said.

"It is my sincerest hope that you didn't study," Ms. Slocum said. "Because otherwise, you are a very disturbed young girl."

"I forgot all about the test," Darcy admitted. "So I just kind of guessed at answers. I did use logic, but I guess it wasn't the right kind."

"I guess not," Ms. Slocum said. "Darcy, I can't ignore this twenty. I'd like to, but it wouldn't be fair to the other students, the ones who did study."

Darcy felt a tear rolling down her cheek.

"Your parents are going to have to know how you

did," Ms. Slocum said. "This is just the kind of test it's all too easy to lose. Bring it back to me tomorrow, with your father or your mother's signature on it."

"All right," Darcy said.

"And if you do a special report for me, on two state capitals and what they're like, I'll drop this grade from your average," Ms. Slocum said. "Any two capitals, one page each, all the facts you can find on them, and don't just copy from the encyclopedia. All right?"

"All right," Darcy said. "I'll do it tonight, I promise."

"No, hand it in on Monday," Ms. Slocum said. "I don't even want to think about you and state capitals for the next couple of days."

"Thank you," Darcy said. She looked up at the clock and saw how late she was for her next class.

"I'll give you a pass," Ms. Slocum said. She wrote out a note for Darcy to give to her math teacher, and then she smiled. "You're a nice girl, Darcy, and a smart one, so I hope this has taught you a lesson. The only way you can really learn something is by studying it."

Darcy nodded. She suspected she already knew that, but she wasn't about to tell Ms. Slocum that.

Darcy avoided telling her friends about how badly she'd done on the test. She wasn't in the mood to be teased. Fortunately, the rest of the school day kept them busy, and by the time the final bell had rung, the only one with her mind on geography was Darcy.

She walked alone to her parents' video shop. It was

better to tell them there, she decided, especially if there were a few customers around. How angry could they get in front of business?

The store was fairly crowded when she arrived, and her parents barely nodded at her. Darcy put her books down in the back office, and went up front. Before she knew it, she was helping out, pulling videos from the shelves, checking people's names off cards. She worked for twenty minutes before she had a chance even to greet her parents, let alone begin her confession.

"It's been like this all day," her mother said. "A constant stream of customers."

"Not that she's complaining," Darcy's father said.

"I'm glad you dropped by to help," Darcy's mother said. "Isabelle was supposed to—" But she didn't even have a chance to finish her sentence before more people walked in.

Darcy looked at her parents. They really were great, hardworking, and nice. They didn't have any of the problems Ms. Slocum asked her about. The worst they'd ever punished her was not letting her have phone calls for an entire weekend.

But then again, the worst Darcy ever did was talk back to them, or whine, or once try to kick a hole through the plywood partition between her room and Isabelle's. They'd never had any real reason to punish her before. It wasn't like she'd brought home twenties all the time.

Darcy thought about her test paper, about how she

hadn't studied for it all weekend long because she'd been too busy planning the party, a party she'd had to talk her parents into in the first place. Her parents thought good grades were really important. They were always going on about study habits, and doing your homework, and getting As and Bs. She remembered once Isabelle had gotten a sixty-seven on a math test, and how angry her father had been. Sixty-seven was over three times better than twenty. Did that mean her father would get more than three times as angry?

And if he did, would that mean no party? Darcy tried to think of other punishments, but that was the one that seemed most likely to her. And without a party, she might lose Sara and Jessica all over again.

Darcy walked to the back office, and pulled out her test paper. The twenty stared right back at her. There really was no need to tell her parents, she thought, at least not right away. She was going to make up the grade anyway, by writing the report. So why upset them now, five days before the party? She could tell them next week, after Ms. Slocum wiped out her grade. They might even laugh at it then, or congratulate Darcy on working hard on her report. Darcy knew it was going to be the best report ever, once she decided which two state capitals to write about.

That still left the problem of getting one of her parents to sign the test. It would be hard to get them to sign without their knowing what it was they were signing.

Darcy looked down at the office desk. There, in front of her, were a half dozen order forms her father had made out, each of them with his signature on it.

Almost as an experiment, she put her test paper on top of one of the order forms. She could see her father's signature through it. It would take no effort at all to trace his name on her test paper.

It was wrong, Darcy knew, but it would also be wrong to cancel the party. She'd have to act fast, in case either of her parents wandered back into the office. So, telling herself to stop shaking, she took out a pen and began to trace.

EIGHT

"I've been working on a code," Darcy told April as they finished putting sheets and blankets on the trundle bed Darcy was to sleep on.

"What for?" April asked.

"For us," Darcy replied. "Your room is right over mine, and if we had a code, we could talk to each other and no one would know."

"You mean like pig latin?" April asked, pulling the pillowcase over the pillow.

"No, a tapping code," Darcy said. "One tap for 'Yes' and two for 'No' and three for 'See you later.'"

April dropped the pillow on Darcy's bed. "Do we really need a code?" she asked. "We see each other every day, and we talk on the phone all the time when we don't see each other."

"This is for late at night," Darcy said.

"Late at night I like to sleep," April said.

"I still think a code's a good idea," Darcy declared. "Something just the two of us would know."

"Isabelle would figure it out pretty quick," April said. "You're not going to be able to tap on your ceiling without her hearing."

"She won't care," Darcy said. "She sleeps through anything."

"So do I," April pointed out. "You could be tapping, and I could be snoring, and you'd think my snores were answering your taps, and I could wake up in the morning and find out I agreed to change my name and run off to Bolivia or someplace."

Darcy sat down on her bed. She didn't always get to sleep over on weekday nights, but her parents had agreed to this Thursday-night visit. Darcy had been glad to have the chance to see April. She'd been so busy with Sara and Jessica, she'd hardly had time for her cousin all week. "I still think we need a code," she said. "You'll like having one once you learn it."

"I have too much to learn already," April said. "I've got a test in French tomorrow and a quiz in math, and next week I have a paper due for social studies."

"Don't say those words," Darcy said. "I never want to think about social studies again."

"I thought you liked social studies," April said.

"I used to," Darcy replied. "But right now I'd rather think about being social. Is everybody still excited about the party?"

"I guess so," April said. "I think they'll be more excited on Sunday, when we actually have it."

"My friends are excited all the time," Darcy said. "They don't just stop and start the way yours do."

"The twins wanted to know if they could bring something," April said. "So I said like what, and Megan said like a merry-go-round. I guess their father owns one, and he lets them use it on special occasions, and they asked him if they could bring it over here, and he said yes."

"Where would we put it?" Darcy asked. "Would it fit in your living room?"

"I think outside," April replied. "Anyway, I told them no, and Megan asked why, so I said we didn't have merry-go-round insurance. Melissa said she thought we'd think it was too babyish but Megan had insisted on asking, which was the first time I ever heard them disagree on anything."

"Would you like having an identical twin?" Darcy asked. She got into bed and pulled the blanket up close to her chin. April had the responsibility of turning the light out, which she promptly did.

"I don't think so," April said. "Before I moved here, I used to wish I had a sister—you know, someone I could share things with."

Darcy laughed. "You've obviously never had a sister," she said. "The only thing I share with Isabelle is a bathroom."

"Yeah, but Isabelle's so much older than you," April

said. "I meant a sister more my age. Sometimes I wished it was a twin. Especially when Mom and Dad split up. I really wished I had a sister then."

"I wish I'd known," Darcy said. "I would have sent you Isabelle."

April whacked at Darcy with her pillow. "Did you ever wish you had a twin?" she asked when they stopped giggling.

"Sure," Darcy said. "All the time. I always figured if there were two of me, I'd stand a better chance against Isabelle."

"I think what we are is better than twins," April said. "I really wouldn't want to be Megan and Melissa and have to dress the same all the time, or even go to the same school. This way if I ever need to talk to someone, I have you, and you have me, and we have our own friends, but we like each other's friends too, and same with parents and even Isabelle, if you know what I mean."

"Also videos," Darcy said. "You can borrow our videos so you don't have to take any out yourself."

"Videos too," April said.

"Do you think we'll borrow each other's boy-friends?" Darcy asked.

"You'd better give me all your leftovers," April replied. "I'm never going to meet any boys at Fairfield."

"Isabelle doesn't date," Darcy said. "But she writes poems about sex anyway."

"She does not," April said.

"Does too," Darcy said. "I read them when she isn't looking. She wrote, 'His tongue was pink like a bouncing ball,' and then she crossed it out and wrote, 'His tongue was red like the burning sun.' Only, she didn't like that, either, so she wrote, 'His tongue was pink like the rising sun.' She crossed that one out too."

"What color is your tongue?" April asked.

"Black," Darcy said, "if I've been eating licorice."

April laughed. "Are you sure writing about tongues is the same as writing about sex?" she asked.

"I think it's as close as Isabelle gets," Darcy replied. "Mom says Isabelle'll date a lot when she goes to college, which won't be a moment too soon as far as I'm concerned. I bet she'll write really dirty poetry then."

"But you won't get to read it," April said.

"Oh, right," Darcy said.

"I wish I could see what color my tongue was," April said. "Right now."

"Turn on the light," Darcy said. "Stick your tongue out and I'll tell you."

"I'd better not," April said. "Mom said lights out ten minutes ago. And it'd be kind of hard to explain to her why we were looking at each other's tongues."

"I'll tell you in the morning then," Darcy said. "Before breakfast."

"Okay," April said. "Darcy, do you really think this party is going to work?"

"What do you mean, work?" Darcy asked.

"Do you think everybody's going to have a good

time?" April said. "Do you think my friends and your friends will get along?"

"Sure," Darcy replied. "Why not?"

"I don't know," April said. "But sometimes I worry about it. It isn't that important to you. I mean, your friends have been your friends for years now, but I'm just getting to know my friends, and if I give a party and it's a disaster, then they won't want to be my friends anymore. And what's worse, they'll tell everybody else at Fairfield, and then nobody'll want to be my friend, and I'll spend the next six years of my life without any friends at all."

"You'll have me," Darcy said. "And you can be friends with my friends."

"I guess," April said. "But I don't think your friends like me all that much. And I want my own, anyway. So this party is really important to me. I wish we'd said yes to the rock band."

"Do you want to call up Mr. Morrow and ask him?" Darcy asked. "I bet he's still awake."

"No," April said. "Because then it's more like the twins' party than ours. Mom says if we just get the girls mingling together in the very beginning, the party will work out, but we have to make sure they do that. Darcy, you have to promise me that you and your friends won't just stay on one side of the room, no matter how my friends act."

"I promise," Darcy said. "How're your friends going to act?"

"I'm not sure," April said. "But sometimes they seem a little scared of the public-school kids."

"My friends are real scary," Darcy said. "But I'll tell them to leave their knives and guns at home."

"I'm not joking," April said. "Your friends have to be nice, Darcy. Tell them they have to be nice."

Darcy remembered Sara's threat to call everybody snobs. She wasn't sure whose side she was on anymore. "My friends'll be nice if yours are," she said. "And if yours aren't, mine won't be."

"We have to make sure they're all nice," April said. "We have to make sure everybody has a great time."

"It's going to be fine," Darcy said. She felt her foot thumping against the mattress. That only happened when she was nervous.

"Promise?" April said.

"Promise," Darcy said.

"Good," April said. She turned her face to the wall, covered half her mouth with her pillow, and muttered, "I feel better. Night, Darcy."

"Night," Darcy said. She lay flat on her back and stared at the ceiling. What if her friends acted up? What if Sara called everyone a snob, or Kristen and Michelle spoke only to each other and Marie sat in a corner feeling shy. That left only Jessica that Darcy could count on, and Jessica might decide to go along with Sara. And what if Sara's curse hadn't worked last weekend because it was waiting for this one, and the curse would be on the whole party and it would be a disaster? Not only would April lose her friends, but Darcy would lose hers, and April would be so mad at her, Darcy would lose her as well, and her entire life would be ruined. Both feet started to thump.

Darcy sat up in bed. She couldn't believe it. She hadn't been worried about the party five minutes earlier, not until April brought it up, and now April was already asleep and Darcy was a nervous wreck. It was so unfair. Darcy didn't know if she'd ever be able to fall asleep again.

The apartment was dark, but Darcy could hear sounds coming from her home downstairs. Her parents were still awake. They were unaware of how close to ruin their younger daughter's life was.

Then again, there was a lot her parents were unaware of, Darcy realized. The thought didn't make her any happier. She stared into the darkness of the bedroom and thought about the forgery. Ms. Slocum hadn't seemed to notice. She hadn't even complained when Darcy handed in her two state-capital reports right away. Darcy couldn't bear the idea of waiting to do them, and had worked hard on them the night before. Jackson, Mississippi, and Cheyenne, Wyoming. She'd used two different encyclopedias and a geography book to make sure she didn't just copy. The reports were good, and that meant the twenty would be wiped out as though it had never happened, and since it had never happened, it didn't matter that Darcy had forged her father's signature. At least, it seemed that way to Darcy. She wasn't about to test her theory on anyone else.

Darcy sighed. She couldn't fall asleep now. It would be hard for her to anyway, knowing her parents were awake downstairs, probably watching some wonderful old movie they'd just gotten in the store. April and Aunt Joanne always went to bed earlier than Darcy's family did. Darcy's mom said that even when they were kids, Joanne needed more sleep.

There was no point sitting on a bed in a dark room listening to April's quiet breathing. So Darcy got up and tiptoed out of the room. Sure enough, all the lights were out. Even Aunt Joanne's room was dark. They were sound asleep, leaving Darcy with no one to talk to and nothing to do.

She knew she could go downstairs and go to sleep in her own bed, but she didn't feel like explaining to her parents why she was suddenly so agitated. It was better to sit quietly in the living room upstairs until she was calm enough or tired enough to face the bed.

Darcy turned a light on and looked around. It was a nice living room, nowhere near as cluttered as her family's room was. April and Aunt Joanne were a lot neater than Darcy's family. Also there were only two of them, which cut the clutter potential in half.

Darcy walked around the room, looking at things much more intently than she ever had before. She had never really had the chance to examine how April and

Aunt Joanne lived, not without them around to see her doing it. They were neat people. Aunt Joanne's papers were on a desk in the living room, but they were lined up so carefully, they almost looked like decoration. In Darcy's house there were piles of paper all over the place, and none of them were neat.

She wandered into the dining room and found April's schoolbooks piled just as carefully on the table. Darcy checked them out. They used the same social-studies textbook and math, but different English books, and, of course, April had French and Spanish books as well. Darcy lifted the books off of April's notebook and opened that up. April's notes and homework were much neater than Darcy's, and there were no twenties to be found. Not that Darcy had hers on display.

She went section by section through the looseleaf, not sure whether what she was doing was right or wrong, but not really caring either. It was comforting to see April's handwriting, to look at her work. Comforting, that is, until she hit English.

"A Pocketful of Love."

"A book report by April Hughes."

Book report! How could Darcy have forgotten? She and April both had book reports due on the same day, on Friday. Tomorrow! Darcy had a book report due tomorrow, and she hadn't even looked at the book. She wasn't even sure she remembered what its title was. Something about videos, which she hadn't wanted to take out, but April had made her because April had wanted to read *A Pocketful of Love* even though Darcy had said she wanted it first. And now April had her book report all neatly done, and Darcy had nothing to hand in, and she had to do something or else she'd get in big trouble in English, and after the big trouble she'd gotten in in social studies, she didn't think she could stand any more trouble ever, much less that week, three days before the party. If her parents found out, they'd be sure to cancel the party, and then April would never speak to her again, let alone Sara and Jessica, and it would be real easy for her parents to find out. All that would have to happen was April asking how Darcy's book report had turned out in front of Darcy's parents, and the truth would come out, and there would go Darcy's entire life.

Darcy stared down at April's book report. How could she have forgotten it was due? Why hadn't April reminded her? Why hadn't April let her take out the book she wanted instead of that boring thing on videos?

But more important, what was Darcy to do? She couldn't go downstairs, sneak into her house, spend the night reading the video book, and then write the report. They were all wide awake there, and they'd ask lots and lots of questions Darcy had no desire to answer. It might be enough that she'd forgotten the report until the last minute to get her parents going. She couldn't take the chance.

Darcy bit down on her thumbnail. There was only one answer she could see, and that was to copy April's report. No one would ever know. The girls went to different schools, and she knew the two English teachers would never get together to compare notes. April wouldn't even have to find out. All Darcy had to do was copy April's report, maybe even changing a word or two, so it was a little more original. Then she could hand the report in, and no one would be the wiser.

Darcy knew that was cheating, and she didn't like being a cheat. She decided that once the party was over, she'd actually read *A Pocketful of Love*. That way it would be okay; she'd have done the work, just not in the ordinary order. She might even write a separate report all her own, if she still felt bad about what she'd done.

She tiptoed back into the living room, got a pen from Aunt Joanne's desk, and turned the light out there. Then, very carefully, she took a sheet of paper out from April's looseleaf, and making sure to use the format her teacher required of her, Darcy began to copy.

NINE

The party was a huge success.

Darcy was delighted (and April amazed) at how well all the girls got along. It was as though twelve strangers had instantly become friends. If you hadn't known which girl went to Fairfield and which to the Middle School, nothing in their behavior would have told you. Sara struck up an immediate conversation with Katie. Kristen and Emily began swapping jokes that the other girls overheard and laughed at as well.

To add to the wonderment of it all, Megan and Melissa showed up in different outfits. Megan had on jeans and a shirt, Melissa was wearing a skirt and blouse.

"We did it so your friends could tell us apart," Megan told Darcy. "We know how scary we must be to strangers."

"That was very thoughtful of you," Darcy said. (April nodded.)

Of course the twins spent most of their time together (you couldn't expect too many miracles at one party), but they talked a lot with Marie and Michelle. The Four Ms, Sara called them, and the nickname stuck for the entire party, especially when Emily demanded to be an Em too. It was silly, Darcy knew, but she couldn't remember ever laughing so hard. (April laughed too.)

Although April and Darcy had prepared tons of food, it seemed to get eaten immediately, but that was all right. Darcy's father, seeing that they'd run out of chips and cookies, ran to the supermarket, and when he came back with fresh supplies, he said, "Caterer's here," and Darcy laughed some more. (So did April.) Darcy then had to explain to everybody why that was so funny, and the girls all laughed at the idea that Darcy's father hadn't known his own wedding was catered. That got them talking about their weddings, what they wanted them to be like. The twins wanted a double wedding, of course, preferably to identical twins. It turned out Marie knew identical twins at her old school, nice boys, she said, perfect for Megan and Melissa, and the twelve of them conspired to find ways the four twins could meet.

And then, as though things weren't going perfectly enough, the doorbell rang, and Darcy opened it to find Mr. Morrow standing on the front porch with Boys Will Be, who were Darcy's absolutely favorite rock group (April's too).

"The Boys were in town, and I happened to run into

them," Mr. Morrow said. "So I invited them here. I hope you don't mind."

"I don't mind at all," Darcy said. She led everybody to the party, and soon Boys Will Be (all five of them) were talking and eating chips and cookies, surrounded by twelve adoring fans.

"We brought our instruments," the lead singer of Boys Will Be said. (What was his name? Darcy felt a brief twinge of unease that she couldn't remember it.) "Would you like us to play?"

"Is there enough room here?" Darcy asked. (Her living room seemed to be getting smaller and smaller. Funny, she thought they'd decided to have the party at April's.)

"How about on your front yard?" Mr. Morrow asked. "Plenty of space there."

So they all trooped out to the front yard, and Darcy was astounded to see that Mr. Morrow had had a little stage set up, and all the Boys Will Be equipment, drums and amps and guitars, was there, and soon the band was playing, and half the block came on over, and people were dancing, and Darcy's friends, and Darcy, and April's friends (and April) were all shrieking and dancing and having an unimaginably good time.

Right after the band finished its third song, Darcy felt someone tapping her on her shoulder. "Darcy Greene?" a man's voice asked.

Darcy turned around to say yes, and discovered it was a police officer.

"I have a warrant for your arrest," he said. "On the charge of forgery."

"What are you talking about?" Darcy asked, but then she saw Ms. Slocum standing by the officer's side.

"She's the one," Ms. Slocum declared. "She forged her father's name."

"No," Darcy said, but the police officer had taken her by the elbow and was starting to lead her away from the party. Only, before they'd gone more than a step, another police officer showed up. A woman this time, and she was accompanied by Mrs. Cohen, Darcy's English teacher.

"Arrest that girl for theft!" Mrs. Cohen cried, pointing her finger at Darcy. "She stole her cousin's book report."

"I'll take her now," the second officer said to the first.

"Sorry," the first one said. "I found her first, so she's mine."

"She's mine," the second one said, and grabbed Darcy by the left arm as the first one held her by her right. They began to pull at Darcy, while the two teachers both screamed, "Arrest her!" and everybody, all Darcy's friends and April's and Darcy's family and Mr. Morrow and Boys Will Be and April herself all began to shout, "Thief! Forger!" and Darcy's mother went up to her and said, "You're no daughter of mine," and her father said, "I hope you get twenty years," and April said, "You stole from me," and Darcy was crying, and everybody was laughing at her, and the officers were pulling so hard she was sure they were about to tear her in two—

"NO!"

"Darcy, what is it? Wake up!"

Darcy opened her eyes. She was in her room, and her mother was sitting on her bed looking terribly worried.

"A dream?" Darcy asked, disappointed at first that Boys Will Be hadn't actually been at her party, then immensely relieved that none of the rest of it had happened either.

"A nightmare," her mother said. "Pre-party jitters, I guess. Come on, honey. It's time for you to get up anyway."

"I dreamt about the party," Darcy said. "It was going so well, and then terrible things happened."

"Nothing terrible's going to happen today," her mother said. "Unless you spend the whole day hiding in bed and not helping April out."

"I'm getting up," Darcy said. Her arms still hurt from being pulled. "Mom, does a bad dream mean a good party?"

"I don't see why not," her mother said. "But the only way to find out is to have the party and see how it goes."

Darcy got out of bed, had breakfast, then went upstairs to help April with the preparations. April was taking cookie sheets out of the oven as Darcy arrived.

"No!" April cried, practically the minute Darcy entered the kitchen. "They're burnt."

"Let me see," Aunt Joanne said. She lifted a cookie with a spatula, then shook her head. "They're goners," she declared. "You might as well bake a whole new batch."

April looked as though she was about to cry. Darcy knew exactly how she felt.

"I had terrible nightmares," Darcy told April as April began sifting flour for the second time that morning. "All I dreamt about was the party."

"I hardly got any sleep," April replied. "Mom says if I'm this nervous every time I have a party, this is the last one she'll ever let me have."

"What about your wedding?" Darcy asked, remembering a fragment from her dream, something about weddings and the twins.

"She says I can elope," April said. "I already asked her."

Darcy laughed. It felt good to be standing there, knowing April was as nervous as she, knowing April loved her and would continue to love her no matter how the party went. It made it easier for Darcy to help out, put out cups and plates and napkins and pour bags of potato chips into bowls and select music for them to listen to (two Boys Will Be cassettes, with no expectations that the real thing would show up). Every time the phone rang in either apartment, the girls crossed their fingers that it wasn't one of their friends canceling, and it never was. By one o'clock everything was set, and by 1:10 the first guest had arrived.

Soon all twelve girls were there, but Darcy was dismayed to see it was nothing like her dream. The twins were, of course, dressed identically, and the only contact the middle school girls seemed to make with them was to giggle at them. So the twins went into a corner by themselves, not even talking with their Fairfield friends. Marie sat by herself also, and the other girls simply paired up, old friend with old friend. The party had Failure written all over it.

"Come on, Sara," Darcy said, sure if she got Sara going, the party would fall into shape. "Talk with the twins. They're really interesting once you get to know them."

"They don't look interesting," Sara declared. "Just weird."

"They do look strange," Jessica said. "Not interested in anyone but themselves."

"Fairfield girls are always just interested in themselves," Sara said. "Rich snobby girls are like that."

Darcy sighed. The last thing the party needed was Sara broadcasting her opinion of Fairfield girls. She edged away from Sara and Jessica, and prayed that April could think of something before open hostilities broke out. Not that April was trying to get her friends to cooperate. She was standing by herself, not talking to anyone. Some co-hostess she was turning out to be.

"I have an idea," April said, just as Darcy had given up all hope. "Well, it's more like a game than an idea."

"A game!" Darcy said. "That's great!" She clapped at the idea, but no one joined her so she stopped. One person applauding sounded really dumb.

"We need two teams," April said. "Middle School and Fairfield. And what we do is, we put our names in a hat—well, I actually have that all ready—and a Middle School girl pulls out a Fairfield name, or vice versa, and asks her a question, like what's her favorite color or subject or something like that, and the other Fairfield girls get to say what they think it is, and then the girl whose name got pulled out says what it really is. Mom and I invented the game last night."

"How do you win?" Jessica asked.

"I don't think you really do," April said. "Mom says it's an icebreaker. That way we can get to know each other a little better."

"Do we have to?" Sara asked.

"Yes," Darcy said, scowling at her best friend.

"Come on," Emily said. "It might be fun."

April offered the hat to the Middle School girls first. Jessica pulled the first name out. It was Megan's. "Tell me, Megan," she said. "What's your favorite color."

"I know that," Melissa said.

"Not fair," Sara said. "She would know. It's probably her favorite color too."

"Melissa, maybe you should skip this round," April said. "I think Megan's favorite color is pink."

"Blue," Emily said.

"Orange," Katie said.

"Yellow," Ashley said.

"It's purple," Megan said.

"I knew that," Melissa said. "Megan's favorite is purple and mine is lavender."

"That's how you can tell us apart," Megan said to the Middle School girls. "Our favorite colors are different."

Sara snorted. Darcy didn't blame her.

"All right, it's our turn," April said. "Katie, pull a name out."

Katie pulled out Marie's name. "What's your favorite color?" she asked.

"I don't know what Marie's favorite color is," Jessica said. "She just started at the Middle School in October."

"I think it's red," Darcy said, because red was her favorite color and she couldn't begin to guess what Marie's might be.

"Blue maybe," Michelle said.

"Purple," Kristen said. "Like Melissa's."

"No," Melissa said. "My favorite color is lavender. Megan's is purple."

"Lavender then," Kristen said.

"I pass," Sara said. "This is too hard a game."

"I don't really have a favorite," Marie said. "I guess if I had to choose though, it would be pink. Or maybe yellow."

Darcy began to pray for the arrival of Mr. Morrow and Boys Will Be.

"I have Emily's name," Sara said. "Emily, what's the thing you're most scared of?"

At least it wasn't colors.

"She's scared of snakes," Megan said.

"Of thunder," Melissa said.

"Of big dogs," April said.

"Of speaking in public," Ashley said.

"Of flying," Katie said.

"Maybe she's scared of boys," Sara said.

"No fair," Katie said. "It isn't your turn to guess."

"I just thought maybe you all went to an all-girls' school because you were scared of boys."

"We're more scared of girls like you," Katie said.

"Is that what Emily's scared of?" Sara asked. "Girls like us?"

"I'm scared of cancer," Emily said. "Are you satisfied?"

"I'll pick next," April said. "I got Darcy." She laughed, but no one else did. "Darcy, what's the worst thing you've ever done?"

Darcy stared at her cousin. She couldn't believe April had asked her that, in front of all their friends, with April's mother in her bedroom, not twenty feet away.

"Darcy hit Billy Mullins once," Michelle said.

"He deserved it," Darcy said.

"And she snitched on me once to Mrs. Mulgrew," Jessica said. "I almost didn't forgive her for that."

"When did I do that?" Darcy asked.

"Two years ago," Jessica said. "When she scolded you for passing notes in class and you said it was my note."

Darcy didn't even remember. She began feeling her cheeks turn bright red.

"She poured salt all over Erica Slade's macaroni once," Kristen said.

"I did that in first grade!" Darcy cried.

"Erica puked," Kristen said. "Practically on top of me."

The other girls laughed, but it wasn't a friendly sound.

"I don't know Darcy very well," Marie said. "But I bet whatever the worst thing she ever did was, it was really awful."

The girls laughed even harder.

"I know the worst thing Darcy ever did," Sara said. "She treated her best friends like dirt when—"

"The worst thing I ever did was forge my father's name on a test," Darcy said.

"When did you do that?" April asked.

"On Wednesday," Darcy said. "And then on Thursday I copied your book report, April, and on Friday I handed it in to my teacher like I'd written it. There. You wanted to know worst. That's worst."

"You stole my book report?" April asked.

"Well, it was your fault," Darcy said. "I wanted to read the book, I said so first, but you said no, I couldn't,

I had to read some stupid book you picked for me, and I didn't want to, so I forgot about it, and then Thursday night when I was sleeping over here you got me so upset I couldn't sleep, so I walked around and I found the book and that reminded me of the book report, and I didn't have time then to read a whole book and write a report on it, so I copied yours. I changed some words, but basically I just copied, and I got a twenty on my social-studies test, so I had to forge Dad's name, and that was your fault too because you didn't give me a chance to study all weekend with all your talk about this stupid party, and I hate you and I hate everybody here and I hate school and it's all your fault. Everything was fine until you moved upstairs!"

"Darcy!" April cried, but Darcy no longer cared. She opened the door to the hallway, ran out of the apartment, down the stairs, out the front door, and kept on running until she knew she could run no longer.

TEN

Darcy sat on her favorite park bench, staring at the pigeons, debating what to do with the rest of her life, when she spotted Isabelle jogging toward her.

At first Darcy thought about running, but then she stayed put. Isabelle had longer legs and, for a poet, made pretty good speed. No matter where Darcy ran, Isabelle would be sure to catch up with her.

"It's a good thing this is a small town," Isabelle said, puffing slightly. "I've been running all over looking for you." She sat down next to Darcy.

"Why?" Darcy asked. Maybe a miracle had happened. Maybe Mr. Morrow had shown up with Boys Will Be.

"Aunt Joanne called to ask me to find you," Isabelle replied. "She said there was a big scene at your party, and you ran out, and she was worried about you."

No miracle. Darcy swallowed hard.

"Want to talk about it?" Isabelle asked.

"No," Darcy said.

Isabelle smiled. "Come on, Darcy," she said. "You love talking. Why are you suddenly taking a vow of silence?"

Darcy stared at her older sister. April, she knew, actually confided in Isabelle on occasion. "Promise you won't write a poem about it?" she asked.

"Promise," Isabelle said. "What happened, Darce?"

"The party was a disaster," Darcy replied. "Everybody hated everybody else. And I knew April was going to hate me if it kept on like that, she practically told me so, and then we started playing this stupid game, which wasn't my idea, it was April's, and we had to confess stuff, and I confessed that I'd kind of cheated this week in school and I didn't want everybody to know that, and April got upset and I got upset and I said some horrible things I didn't really mean and I ran out. Now you know. Satisfied?"

"You kind of cheated in school?" Isabelle said. "What does 'kind of cheated' mean?"

"It means I got a twenty on my geography test and I didn't tell Mom and Dad and I forged Dad's signature on the test paper, and then I didn't do my book report and I copied April's instead and handed that in," Darcy replied.

"Yeah," Isabelle said. "I'd say that's kind of cheated."

"And now everybody knows," Darcy said. "I told

them all. And Aunt Joanne must know. She must have heard everything, and she'll tell Mom and Dad, and I had a horrible nightmare that I was arrested for cheating."

"I don't think that'll happen," Isabelle said. "But you know you have to tell Mom and Dad the truth."

"I know," Darcy said. "But couldn't I wait a few years?"

Isabelle shook her head. "People who talk a lot should never cheat," she declared. "It's just bad policy."

"It was the perfect crime too," Darcy said, and then she managed a little giggle. "Both of them."

Isabelle laughed. "You have quite a future as a criminal," she said. "But only after you take that vow of silence."

"What'll Mom and Dad do to me?" Darcy asked.

"I don't know," Isabelle said. "The worst I ever confessed to them was I wore one of Mom's dresses playing dress-up and ripped the hem. I remember I was terrified to tell her, but I did."

"How'd she punish you?" Darcy asked.

"She taught me how to sew," Isabelle said with a shudder. "Needle and thread and all that. I vowed never to wear clothes again."

"You're wearing clothes now," Darcy said.

"I broke my vow," Isabelle replied. "Mom and Dad are both at the store. You want to go over there and get it over with?"

"No," Darcy said, but she got up anyway. "I've always been good," she said. "I've never done anything really wrong in my life, and this week I've done everything wrong and now nobody's speaking to me."

"I'm speaking to you," Isabelle said.

"April won't be," Darcy said. "She's going to live upstairs from me for the rest of my life and never say another word to me ever."

"You'll have to work that out with April," Isabelle declared. "Your first step is to work things out with Mom and Dad."

Darcy knew Isabelle was right, something she had never before assumed about her older sister. The two girls walked together to their parents' store.

"I'm not going to go in with you," Isabelle said. "Just remember to explain everything and be completely honest, and if all else fails, start crying."

Darcy nodded. Isabelle bent over and gave her a quick kiss on the cheek. "It's okay," Isabelle said. "Everybody still loves you." She smiled at her younger sister, then walked away.

Darcy took a deep breath. Video To Go, unfortunately, was empty. Just her parents, no customers to hide behind. She gave brief thought to running again, but decided she might as well get it over with. The happy part of her life had ended; now came pain and suffering. She only hoped she could use the pain and suffering to make herself an even greater great film director.

"Hi, Mom," she said. "Dad."

"Darcy," her father said. "Aren't you having a party?"

"I was," Darcy replied. "I kind of left it."

"Why'd you do that?" her father asked. Darcy's mother also looked concerned.

Darcy looked at her parents. They were such nice people. It would probably break their hearts to have to throw her out on the street.

"I have something to tell you," Darcy said. "Well, actually I have a lot to tell you."

"Sit down, honey," her mother said, and Darcy took one of the stools behind the counter. "Whatever happened, I'm sure it can't be as bad as all that."

"I think it is, Mom," Darcy said, and then she began crying. It felt good to cry, and she had so much to cry about. Darcy's mother located a box of tissues from the office, and handed some tissues to her. Darcy blew her nose a few times and waited for her parents to forgive her.

"We still need to know what happened," her father said.

Darcy blew her nose again. Parents definitely were tough. "I did lots of wrong things this week," she said. "And I know you're going to hate me, and April already does."

"We won't hate you," her mother said. "But we need to know what you mean by wrong things."

Darcy sighed deeply. She remembered a week's worth

of lies, saying she'd done her homework when she hadn't, claiming the test was a surprise quiz, telling her parents she'd done fine. If Darcy ever went into a life of crime, she was sure she'd rob banks. Only the big-time stuff for her.

"I guess there were a couple of really big things," she said. If her parents wanted to find out about the little things, they could just grill her. "I flunked that geography test I took. The state-capital one."

"And you said you passed it," her mother said. "Darcy, you should know better than to lie about something like that."

"We all flunk tests occasionally," her father said. "Just don't make a habit of it."

"Ms. Slocum wanted your signature on it," Darcy said. "On account of I got a twenty."

"A twenty!" her father said.

Darcy nodded. "I thought Kansas City was the capital of Missouri," she said.

"So did I," her father said.

"It isn't," Darcy said. "But that got me started off wrong, and then I used logic, and you know what? If you start off wrong, then logic only makes you wronger."

"I don't remember your asking either of us to sign that test," her mother said.

"That's because I forged Dad's signature," Darcy replied. "I'm not sure, but that may have been the worst thing I did this week."

"What's the competition?" her father asked.

Darcy longed for a customer to come in and interrupt the flow of the conversation. But everybody was obviously at home, watching the tapes they had already taken out. "Remember that book report I had to do?" she said to her mother.

Her mother nodded.

"Well, I forgot it," Darcy said. "I didn't even think about it until Thursday night when I was at April's, and by then it was too late to read a book and write a report."

"So you copied off the book jacket?" her father asked.

"No," Darcy said. "You know, that never occurred to me."

Darcy's father cleared his throat. "It's a bad practice," he said. "Basically cheating. And you almost always get caught."

"What did you do, Darcy?" her mother asked as Darcy considered how many times her father must have copied from the book jacket.

"What?" Darcy said, still thinking about her father's life of crime, and how she seemed to have inherited all his dishonest genes. "I copied April's book report and I handed it in as mine." She smiled at her father, sure he'd understand.

"You did what?" her father said. He didn't sound understanding at all.

"I knew I'd get away with it," Darcy said. "April

would never know and neither would my teacher, and I would have gotten away with it, and everything else, except at the party I told everybody everything, and then I ran out, and I know April hates me, and I bet you do too." She felt like crying again.

"I just don't understand," her mother said. "Darcy, you had to have known that what you did was wrong."

Darcy nodded.

"So why did you do it?" her mother asked.

Darcy sniffled. Her mother silently handed her another tissue.

"I don't know," Darcy said. "I guess I was afraid if I told you about the twenty, you'd make me cancel the party, and I knew how important the party was to April." She took a deep breath. "No, that isn't true either," she said. "It was important to me. Sara and Jessica were mad at me last week. They said I spent all my time with April and no time with them anymore, and I thought they weren't going to be my friends unless I did something wonderful for them, like having a party, and then we made up, but I had to spend time with them or else they'd get mad at me again, and I totally forgot about the geography test, and then I totally forgot about the book report, and I'm not a cheater, really I'm not. I've never copied on a test, and I hate people who do, and at the party everybody was saying the worst thing I ever did, and Sara was about to say something to make April feel bad, and I had to shut her up, so I told everybody about the twenty and the book report, and then I got so mad I blamed it all on April." Darcy felt tears running down her cheeks, but she just brushed them off.

"Wow," her mother said. "What a mess."

Darcy nodded.

"I suppose you want us to say you've suffered enough," her father said. "Worrying and ruining your party."

"That would be nice," Darcy said. She managed a smile.

"The problem is, you haven't," her father said. "Sure, you've suffered. But not enough."

"First of all, you have to tell your teachers what you've done," her mother said. "We can't let you get away with it at school."

Darcy nodded. "I know," she said. She did, too.

"And whatever punishment your teachers give you, you're going to have to accept without griping," her mother said. "You're going to abide by their rules."

"All right," Darcy said.

"We're going to have to check on your homework for a while," her father said.

"But that's so babyish," Darcy said. "You know I do it."

"We used to know you did it," her father said. "But you're going to have to prove it to us all over again."

"You need to get your priorities back in order," her mother said. "No phone calls for a week, no visits either. Just school, and home. No late-night movies with us, for that matter."

"I have to talk to April," Darcy said. "I have to make it up with her."

"All right," Darcy's mother said. "You can speak to April either in person or on the phone, to apologize and patch things up. But that's it until a week from Monday."

"And we want you to think about all the wrong things you did," her father said. "Especially that forgery, and how actions like that can hurt a lot of people."

"Think how badly you've hurt yourself," her mother said. "You thought you'd get away with those crimes, and you didn't. And now your parents are angry at you, and April's angry at you, and your teachers are about to be. Was it worth it, Darcy?"

Darcy shook her head.

"The store's quiet now," her mother said. "Bill, you keep an eye on it while I walk Darcy home."

"No," Darcy said. "Not yet. I'm not ready to go home. Can't I stay here?"

"In the office," her mother said. "For a little while."

Darcy accepted her self-imposed exile and sat quietly in the office. She could hear the customers coming in, could make out snatches of conversation. She usually loved talking with the customers, helping them out with their choices. But today she was just as happy to remain in hiding.

Her parents let her have an hour in the office before her mother came to get her. "You'd better go home now," she said. "Come on, honey. You know you're not through with your apologizing."

Darcy nodded. She followed her mother out of the shop and walked silently back with her to their home.

"Do I have to go upstairs?" Darcy asked as they reached the front door. There were no signs of a rock band on the lawn. None of her dream had come true, but she felt just as miserable anyway.

"You can call her," her mother said.

"Thank you," Darcy said. She walked into the kitchen and dialed April's number. She could hear the phone ringing upstairs.

"Hello?"

"Hi, Aunt Joanne," Darcy said. "Is April around?"

"I'm glad you're home," her aunt said. "Let me see how April's feeling."

Darcy waited a few moments, and then her aunt got back on the line. "April's still upset," she said. "I think you should try talking to her tomorrow, instead."

"I'm not sure if I can," Darcy said. "I think I'm only allowed one phone call."

Darcy's mother took the phone from Darcy. "Jo, this is Karen," she said. "April's still that angry? All right. No, of course Darcy can call again tomorrow. We've cut off her phone privileges, but we do want her to apologize to April. Fine. I'll tell her that." She hung up the phone and looked at her daughter. "Tomorrow after school," she said. "April will call you if she's ready."

Darcy nodded. "Do you think she'll forgive me?" she asked.

"I don't know," her mother said. "But I think you'd better make a list of all the things you have to apologize to her for in the meantime."

ELEVEN

Darcy got to school a half hour early on Monday. Whatever explanations she had to make, she wanted to get over with before her friends could find her.

She went to Ms. Slocum's room first, and was relieved to see her behind her desk. Darcy didn't know whether or not to knock, so she just walked in.

"Hello, Darcy," Ms. Slocum said. "If you're here to ask me about the extra report you did, I read it over the weekend, and it was fine. I erased the twenty from your record."

"Thank you," Darcy said. "That is sort of what I wanted to talk to you about."

"Sort of?" Ms. Slocum asked.

Darcy grimaced. "The thing is— well, my parents said I had to talk to you, but they were right. I mean, I probably wouldn't if they hadn't told me I had to, but they really are right, so I am, if you know what I mean."

"Darcy," Ms. Slocum said. "You're making as much sense as Oklahoma City being the capital of Kansas."

"You know, my father thought Kansas City was the capital of Missouri too," Darcy said.

"It isn't," Ms. Slocum replied. "No matter what you and your father might think."

"I know," Darcy said. "The thing is, I didn't tell them about the twenty, not until yesterday, and I forged my father's signature on the test, and that's what I had to tell you. I'm sorry. It was wrong, and I'm very sorry. I did the report all on my own though, and I didn't copy from an encyclopedia."

"You forged your father's signature?" Ms. Slocum said.

Darcy nodded.

"That was wrong," Ms. Slocum said. "I can't simply let you get away with that, no matter how sorry you feel."

Darcy nodded again.

"We all make mistakes," Ms. Slocum said. "We all make big mistakes on occasion, like getting a twenty. The important thing is to face up to our mistakes and rectify them. I gave you that chance, Darcy. But you ran away from your failure, didn't you?"

"I didn't face up to it," Darcy said. "I was scared my parents wouldn't let me have a party if they knew about my grade." Now that she thought about it, not having the party would have been the best thing that ever could have happened.

"I think that twenty should go back on your record," Ms. Slocum said. "I'm going to put it back in, and it will affect your average, Darcy. It won't matter that you did that extra report. That's what my punishment is going to be for your forgery. And I'm going to send a note to your parents, explaining that, and I want both of them to sign the note, so I'll know they understand. All right?"

"All right," Darcy said.

"Very well," Ms. Slocum said. "What you did was wrong, and we've agreed on an appropriate punishment. I want you to learn from your mistakes, but not to let them get you down. It's Monday, and you have a lot of things left to learn this week." She smiled at Darcy, who tried hard to smile back.

"Thank you," Darcy said. "May I be excused now?"

"Certainly," Ms. Slocum said. "I'll give you the note after class today."

Darcy thanked her again, and walked down the hall to Mrs. Cohen's room. Mrs. Cohen was standing by the window, staring out. She looked so dreamy, Darcy was sorry to interrupt her.

"Excuse me," Darcy said. "I have to talk to you."

"Certainly, Darcy," Mrs. Cohen said with a smile. "Come on in."

"I have to talk to you about my book report," Darcy said.

"I haven't read them yet," Mrs. Cohen said. "I know I should have over the weekend, but to be perfectly honest, we had unexpected visitors, and things got so hectic, I just put them aside and never got to them. Why? Did you want to change something in yours?"

"I wanted to change everything," Darcy said. "The thing is, I didn't exactly write my book report."

"I don't understand," Mrs. Cohen said.

Darcy wished her teachers had telepathic powers. Explaining things only got more painful the more you did it. "I copied my cousin's report," Darcy said. "My cousin April. She lives upstairs and she goes to Fairfield and she's in seventh grade too, and she had a book report due on Friday, and I forgot about my report and I just copied hers. She didn't know anything about it. The book she took out of the library looked better than the one I did, but I didn't read either of them, so I don't really know. I'm sorry."

"You stole your cousin's book report?" Mrs. Cohen said.

"Yeah," Darcy said. "I mean, yes, I did."

"Oh, Darcy," Mrs. Cohen said. "Why?"

Darcy considered explaining that once you'd embarked on a life of crime, you might as well commit as many crimes as you could possibly get away with, but she didn't think that would be a satisfactory explanation. "I was giving a party on Sunday," she said instead. "And I was afraid if my parents found out I'd forgotten about my book report, they wouldn't let me have the party."

"But why did you forget in the first place?" Mrs. Cohen asked. "Didn't I remind the class?"

"I'm sure you did," Darcy said. "Everyone else remembered. I was just distracted all week because of the party."

"I understand," Mrs. Cohen said. "I was distracted too this weekend. Darcy, you know what you did was wrong, don't you?"

"Oh, yes," Darcy said. "I even had a nightmare you got the police to arrest me. And that was before I told everyone the truth."

"Your parents know?" Mrs. Cohen asked.

Darcy nodded.

"And they're punishing you?" Mrs. Cohen asked.

"No phone calls for a week," Darcy said. "And they're checking my homework until I'm forty."

"All right then," Mrs. Cohen said. "I'm going to take the book report you copied and tear it up. I expect you to hand me a new report on Wednesday. I'll mark it as late, but that's it, as long as you actually read the book and write a good report on it. Do you understand?"

"I'll read it," Darcy said. "I'm never going to cheat again on anything."

"Good," Mrs. Cohen said. "Those are words to live by, Darcy."

Darcy thanked her English teacher and left the room. Two battles down, a few more to go.

The next round came at lunchtime. Darcy sat by

herself, but was joined almost immediately by Sara and Jessica.

"Did you really do all that stuff?" Sara asked as soon as she put her tray down.

"I did," Darcy said. "And I told my parents and Mrs. Cohen and Ms. Slocum and everybody's punishing me, and none of it was April's fault."

"All right," Sara said. "You don't have to bite my head off."

"I have to bite somebody's," Darcy muttered, but Sara didn't hear her.

"I tried calling you last night," Jessica said. "But your mother said you weren't allowed any phone calls for a week."

"I'm not," Darcy said. "Not even from April. The only time I'll get to do anything social is during lunch."

Sara smiled. "You mean you'll be talking to us more this week than to April?" she asked.

Darcy wasn't sure April would ever talk to her again. "I guess so," she said. "My parents can't stop me from talking to you during lunch."

"That's great," Sara said.

"I'll always talk to you during lunch," Darcy said. "And I'll try to do more stuff with you after school. It's just been hard, having April around and having you around too. I have to learn how."

"We'll teach you," Sara said.

"We'll try to be patient," Jessica said. "Do you really like April's friends?"

"They're okay," Darcy said. "Some of them are nice."

"Do you like them more than us?" Jessica asked.

"Of course not," Darcy said. "You're my best friends."

"Good," Sara said. "Just try to remember that."

"I will," Darcy said. "Just as long as you remember that I love April."

"Okay," Sara said. "As long as she doesn't have lunch with us."

Darcy smiled. She knew that was the best she could hope for, and at least for the moment, it would do.

She managed to get through the school day fairly easily after that. It felt good to concentrate on her classes again. Darcy was astounded at how much had gotten taught the week before that she apparently was unaware of. She knew she had a lot of studying to catch up with, but she certainly had the week to do the catching.

She walked home after school, thinking about stopping in at her parents' store, then deciding against it. She knew her parents wanted her to go straight home so she could do her schoolwork. And she had that book to read and the report to write. The only reason for not going straight home was because she was so scared of what April might say.

She unlocked the door to the house and found April sitting on the inside staircase that led to her apartment. "I've been waiting for you," April said. "I didn't know if you could have visitors, so I decided to wait here."

"Thank you," Darcy said. "I guess it's okay for us to meet in the hallway."

"I was real angry at you," April said.

Darcy nodded. She put her books on the floor, and sat on the stairs five down from April. "I said terrible things," she said. "You were right to be angry."

"Okay," April said. "I wanted to make sure you knew that."

"I did," Darcy said. "I knew it even while I was saying it. None of it was your fault. Not really. It's just I like you so much and it's so great having you live here that I kind of forgot about everything else like my friends and school. But it's not your fault you're funny and nice and live upstairs."

"Thank you," April said. "I mean, for thinking I'm funny and nice."

"Well, you are," Darcy said. "Do you think you'll ever forgive me?"

"I talked to my mother about that," April said. "After everybody left. Which they did practically the minute you ran out, you know."

"No, I didn't," Darcy said. "My friends kind of avoided talking to me about the party at school."

"It was an awful party," April said. "It was the absolutely worst party in the history of parties, I think. And I wanted it to be perfect. That's why I made up that game. So that everybody would get to know each other and the party would be perfect."

"I'm sorry," Darcy said. She figured she'd apologized so often in the past twenty-four hours, she might as well change her name to I. M. Sorry.

"I never wanted to speak to you again," April said. "I even told Mom that. I said we had to move away from this house so I'd never see you again. Only, Mom said no."

"Moms always say no to stuff like that," Darcy said.

"I know," April said. "But that's how mad I was. That's why Mom talked to me. She said I was an only child, so I didn't know much about having a sister, and in a lot of ways you were my sister now, so I had all this catching up to do. She said she and your mother used to have terrible fights and throw things at each other and scream they never wanted to see each other again, and now they were sharing a house and they both loved it, but I didn't know about the angry part and the making up part because you and I had been on our best behavior since I moved here, so we'd never really gotten angry before."

"I wasn't really mad at you yesterday," Darcy said. "I was mad at everybody and everything and mostly at me."

"Mom said that was probably it," April said. "She told me I didn't have to be friends with you just because we lived in the same house and were cousins and were the same age. She said my friends certainly didn't have to be your friends, and your friends certainly didn't have to be my friends, and your friends and my friends absolutely certainly didn't have to be friends with each other."

"Good," Darcy said. "The part about friends I mean. I want us to be friends."

"I do too," April said. "And I'm sure your friends are very nice, but I have enough problems making friends with the girls at Fairfield without taking on your friends as well. Half the time I can't tell Megan apart from Melissa, and they're practically my best friends at school. So maybe next time we have a party, you can just invite your friends, or I'll just invite mine, but we won't invite everybody all at once. Except for boys, that is."

"Okay," Darcy said. "They still are your friends, aren't they? They don't blame you because the party was a disaster, do they?"

"They were very understanding," April said. "At school today, Emily and Ashley and Katie all said how hard it must be for me having to practically live with you. They all invited me to their houses for supper and the weekend."

"What about the twins?" Darcy asked.

"They were different," April said. "They told me that once they'd actually gotten into a fight, and they'd both been so angry they'd run into their rooms and slammed their doors and decided they'd never talk to each other again, but it hurt them so much, they made up, and they said I was real lucky to have you and I'd be crazy to stay angry at you. That's really why I waited for you. I know everything Mom said was right about sisters and fighting, but it felt more right when Megan and Melissa said it.''

''I never want to fight again,'' Darcy said.

''Me neither,'' April said. ''But Mom says we will anyway. I'll have to tell her about Megan and Melissa tonight.''

Darcy looked at her watch. ''I should go in,'' she said. ''Mom and Dad said I could make up with you, but that's it. And I guess we've made up.''

''I guess so,'' April said. ''A whole week I can't talk to you or visit you. It doesn't seem fair.''

''You'll spend the week with your friends,'' Darcy said. ''I'll spend it doing homework. I'm sorry about stealing your book report, April.''

''I only got a C-plus on it,'' April said. ''I guess I was so distracted all week long, I didn't work hard enough on it. How did it do at your school?''

''I don't know,'' Darcy said. ''Mrs. Cohen didn't get around to reading it. She said she'd just tear it up, and I'd have to do a new one.''

''The book wasn't very good,'' April said. ''But I still have it, if you want to read it.''

''That's okay,'' Darcy said. ''I'll stick with that video book. There's probably something in it I can learn.''

''Okay,'' April said. ''A whole week. No visits, no phone calls.''

''We can tap,'' Darcy said. ''One for yes and two for no.''

"Okay," April said. "How about if I tap once at night to ask if you're okay, and then you can tap one back or two, and then you can tap one to ask if I'm okay, and I'll tap back one or two."

"Great," Darcy said. "And we can write letters. We don't have to mail them. We can just leave them in our mailboxes."

"And we can put questions in them that the other one can answer that night with taps," April said. "Like if you know I'm going to have supper at Katie's, you can write me that you're going to tap asking if I had a good time, and then I can tap one or two back."

"Great," Darcy said. "In the letters we can work out a better code. Like two shorts and three longs mean I passed my test."

"And two shorts and two longs mean I'm going crazy," April said.

"And one long and one short mean I miss you," Darcy said. "I'm going to, April."

"I'll miss you too," April said. "But it's only for a week. And by the end of the week, we'll have the code all worked out, so no matter whatever happens to us, we'll be able to communicate."

"I'm going in right now to start on my first letter," Darcy said. "After I read my book and do my homework, that is."

"I can't wait to read it," April said. "Darcy, no matter what, we're best cousins."

Darcy grinned. "Best cousins," she said. "Forever."

ABOUT THE AUTHOR

Susan Beth Pfeffer, who has lots of noisy cousins, lives in Middletown, New York. She graduated from New York University with a degree in television, motion picture, and radio studies. She is the author of *April Upstairs,* the companion book to *Darcy Downstairs.* She is also the author of many acclaimed young adult novels, including *Most Precious Blood, Family of Strangers,* and *The Year Without Michael,* which was an ALA Best Book for Young Adults and a *Publishers Weekly* Best Book of the Year.

THE BEST OF SKYLARK

☐ **BIG RED** by Jim Kjelgaard
0-553-15434-6 $2.99/$3.50 in Canada
Danny and an Irish setter named Red form a special
bond as they struggle for survival in the harsh wilderness
of the Wintapi.

☐ **THE INCREDIBLE JOURNEY** by Sheila Burnford
0-553-15616-0 $3.99/not available in Canada
Three house pets, two dogs and a cat, face starvation,
exposure and wild forest animals to make their way
home to the family they love.

☐ **SEAL CHILD** by Sylvia Peck
0-553-15868-6 $3.50/$3.95 in Canada
One summer Molly comes across a slain mother seal,
and meets a mysterious girl named Meara. Nothing can
prepare her for the strange truth...or for the dramatic
event that's about to change their lives—and their friend-
ship—forever.